DUKE OF DARING

LORDS OF SCANDAL

TAMMY ANDRESEN

Keep up with all the latest news, sales, freebies, and releases by joining my newsletter!

www.tammyandresen.com

Hugs!

UNTITLED

The Duke of Daring
Lords of Scandal

By Tammy Andresen

Dear Reader,

Thank you so much for choosing The Duke of Daring. I know you have a lot of choices! While this is a stand-alone book, to enhance your reading experience, I'd recommend downloading the free prologue to the series, *Lords of Scandal*. Not only will it give you a little romance with Emily and Jack's story, but it will introduce you to the cast of characters in *Lords of Scandals*. All my best and happy reading!

Love,
    Tammy

CHAPTER ONE

"DRAT. IT'S RAINING AGAIN." Emily huffed as she stood at the window, staring and frowning deeply.

Minnie Chase crossed the room and brushed back Emily's hair. The woman had a serious case of pre-wedding jitters. Never having been married, Minnie didn't quite understand it, but two days ago, when she'd suggested that Emily simply calm herself, her cousin had burst into a shower of tears. Minnie hadn't made the suggestion again. Rather, she'd taken to whispering near-nonsensical words into her cousin's ear. "This is England, Em. It's always raining. At least the garden will be lush for the day of the ceremony."

"Lush, yes. That's a good point." Emily relaxed against Minnie, her brown hair brushing Minnie's bright red locks. "You've been such a comfort,

Minnie. Thank you. After what happened last week, I've grown so worried that this wedding won't happen."

Minnie winced. That was an excellent point and explained a great deal about Emily's jitters. Minnie rather agreed, in fact if she were in Emily's place, she wouldn't be marrying the man at all.

Last week, Emily, along with Minnie and her sister, Ada, and Emily's sisters, Diana and Grace, had gone to a secret gaming hell called the Den of Sins. There, they'd discovered that Jack, along with five of his friends, ran a secret gaming hell and used the proceeds to pad their fortunes.

Minnie's gut clenched as she remembered that night. The men had been none too happy to have their secret discovered by ladies of society. One in particular had irritated Minnie beyond belief. Daring, they'd called him, but she knew him as The Duke of Darlington. Just thinking his name caused goose pimples to rise on her flesh.

But worse than meeting an errant duke, Emily and Jack had almost cancelled their wedding. "The nuptials are going to happen. Jack said he would retire from the club and that you were what was important." She gave Emily a squeeze.

Emily nodded against her shoulder. "You're right. I just…I can't…I seem to be filled with doubt."

Minnie gave Emily's back a tiny pat and then she let her cousin go. "I know. It's only a month until the wedding and then you can cease worrying." An entire month of keeping Emily constant company. Not that she was completing the task alone. But still. She sighed. It was going to be the longest thirty days of her life.

Emily gave an absent nod, then turned to look through the rain-streaked window. Minnie knew Em wouldn't reply. She'd already retreated back into her worried thoughts. Something she did with more and more frequency as the wedding drew closer.

"Perhaps," she touched Emily's arm, "we could arrange an outing this evening. Aunt Melisandre is hosting an intimate dinner. We could go so you have something to take your mind off the wedding."

Emily waved, not looking at Minnie. "I couldn't possibly. I'm a wreck."

Minnie looked up at the ceiling. No denying that. "Perhaps I could write to Jack. See if he could escort you?"

"Jack?" Emily's full attention focused back on Minnie. "What a marvelous idea. We could go together. When I'm with him, I forget to be afraid."

Minnie's insides fluttered. Emily was the perfect example of why a woman needed to use her head and not her heart when she selected a husband. Not that Minnie needed an example. She'd fallen in love last season only to have her hopes and dreams dashed. Emily only confirmed her worst fears. While she knew Emily loved Jack from the first instant their eyes met, there had been secrets and lies and now a whole heaping pile of uncertainty. "All right then. I'll write him now."

Minnie crossed the room and sat at the desk. Dipping the quill into the ink, she pulled out a fresh piece of parchment from the top drawer. Then she took out the quill again and perched the utensil above the paper. Instead of writing, however, her own mind drifted.

How to choose a husband had dominated her thoughts of late. Minnie had reached one and twenty years of age, past time to be married. And her younger sister Ada was ready for her first season. Which meant that Minnie needed to find a husband or place herself on the shelf. The very idea of Minnie becoming a spinster sent their mother into a dead faint.

Minnie wasn't sure how she felt on the topic. On the one hand, she couldn't quite picture being alone her entire life. On the other, however, she tried to visualize the man who would tolerate her for the rest of his life.

She rested her chin on her other hand. Minnie

had a tendency to tell men exactly what she thought of them, precisely when she thought it. A trait that had frightened more than one suitor away.

Looking down, she realized the parchment now had a giant blotch of black ink dead in the center of the page. She let out a sigh and pulled out a fresh piece, penning a note to Jack.

LORD EFFINGTON,

LADY EMILY CHASE requests the honor of your presence at the home of the Countess of Wilmington's dinner soiree this evening. She finds herself in need of a diversion.

MINNIE STOPPED, frowning with one side of her mouth. Did that sound right? It was true, of course, but perhaps it was too forward? She shook her head. When had she started questioning herself? Probably about the time her father had insisted she find a husband this season or he'd find one for her. Her mother concurred. They were aligning against her.

· · ·

THANK you for your attention to this matter. We hope to see you this evening.

KIND REGARDS,
Miss Minerva Chase

SHE DUSTED the paper and then carefully folded the note, rising again to ring the bell. Attending the ball would do her good as well. Not only would it give her a break from Emily's nervous melancholy but it might give her an opportunity to find a suitor before her father had the chance.

————

LORD DARTAGNAN DARLINGTON, The Duke of Darlington, sat across from his closest friend, ally, and companion through many a lurid tryst and tried to keep his poker face in place. Jack knew him better than anyone, which made lying to his friend exceptionally difficult. "Do you have any plans with Emily between now and the wedding?" he asked, attempting to keep his voice light.

Which was odd in and of itself. He had a naturally deep and rumbling baritone much more suited to thinly veiled threats than to light banter about ladies.

Jack squinted an eye. "Odd question." His friend turned his head to the side. "Daring," he asked, using Dartagnan's nickname at the club.

Actually, Jack had a nickname too, Effing. But Tag had known Jack since before the club and somehow, he'd always thought of the Lord of Effington as just Jack. "What?"

"Are you feeling all right? You're not acting like yourself."

Tag snapped his teeth together. This was not going the way he'd planned. He needed to redirect the conversation quickly. "I'm fine. The last time I saw Emily, however, she threatened to call off the wedding. I'm concerned for you."

Jack grimaced as he looked down. "Right. Thanks for reminding me."

Tag's gut clenched with guilt. He'd wanted to distract Jack, not hurt him. When Emily had walked into the back room of their secret club with her sisters and cousins in tow, their livelihood, at least the fun part of it, had been jeopardized. If word got out they ran the club, it would ruin the mystery that surrounded their identities and could cost them patrons and coin.... One of Den of Sins' greatest assets was the mystery that surrounded its owners.

TAMMY ANDRESEN

Men theorized they were pirates, highwaymen, or cutthroats. No one ever concocted a story that declared the club run by a duke and his fellow peers. "Sorry, chap. I was just worried. You've patched things up with her?"

Jack splayed his fingers on the desk. "More or less." He cleared his throat. "But she's been exceptionally nervous and her sisters and cousins—" Jack's head popped up. "Who you've obviously met."

Tag gave a curt nod trying to disguise that the sisters and cousins were the exact reason he'd come. "I vaguely remember them."

Jack cocked a brow. "Oh please. Flames ignited between you and Minnie."

He snorted despite himself. "Those weren't flames. It was just her bright red hair." Fiery shades of copper as glaring as her personality.

It was Jack's turn to snort. "Daring. I know when you're attracted to a woman."

Tag lowered his brow, leaning forward. "This time you misunderstand. It was not attraction. I was honestly stunned and appalled by the woman. A more flamboyant example of feminine attributes has never crossed my path."

Jack pushed back in his chair, arching a brow. "More flamboyant than the group of gypsies you hired one year for my birthday? More garish than the troop of actresses you brought to—"

"Point made," Tag grated. "They were women of a different cloth. Minnie, as you called her, is the granddaughter of an earl. She should a have more sedated decorum."

Jack stared at him for a moment before he shook his head. "I agree on that point. There is little that is sedated about Minnie. She does everything with a great deal of zest, energy, and enthusiasm. Even verbally sparring with dukes."

Tag's mouth went annoyingly dry. Because he thought of one activity in particular where zest, energy, and enthusiasm would play out nicely. The acts he pictured also involved that mane of glowing hair trailing down her shoulders and onto his, spilling across his pillow. For a moment, his eyes closed.

After the ladies had left the club that evening, Jack had gone with them. The rest of their friends and fellow club owners had stayed behind. That's when the five men had decided they needed to make sure Emily's family did not disclose their secret gaming hell. And so they'd devised a plan. Each of them would watch one of the ladies to ensure she was trustworthy. A fact-finding endeavor.

One of their friends, Exile, a brawny Scot with a

noble heart, had insisted they keep their activities appropriate. If they didn't, he'd personally see them escorted to the altar. And Tag couldn't have that yet. He'd marry eventually, of course, to some simple girl who bore him a few children and didn't ask too much of him emotionally or otherwise. A woman like Minnie was too spirited, too like the woman who'd nearly wrecked his life and his soul six years before.

And Jack. He didn't know anything about their plan. If he found out they were actively following his bride's family…

"So you and Emily are back on good footing? I only ask because what happens with your matrimonial pursuits affects all of us."

Jack glowered. "Even if she cancelled the wedding, she wouldn't share your secrets. I picked a kind and honorable woman. It's why she's so damn offended we run a gaming hell called the Den of Sins."

"She's offended you've lied to her." Tag fired back before he'd weighed the words.

Jack winced. "True. Anyway. Plans continue, but she is nervous. She seems to grow more so the longer we're separated. It would be so much easier if I could just bring her here with me then I'm certain her fears will vanish."

Tag rubbed the back of his neck. He needed the wedding to happen. For Jack's sake, of course. But also for his own. He'd chosen Minnie to watch over. More because she deserved a good measure of humility and he intended to give it to her. She'd been openly rude to him the one occasion they'd met. In order to do that, however, he needed an opportunity to see her. "Anything I can do?"

A knock sounded at the door. The butler walked in carrying a tray with a letter upon it. "Forgive the interruption, my lord, but an urgent letter has arrived for you."

Jack removed the letter from the tray and tore it open, then scanned the contents. "Thank you, Beasley." He passed the letter to Tag. "There's nothing I need. Unless you know how to calm restless women. Emily is feeling especially concerned after all that's happened, and I'm afraid she's causing the rest of the ladies to worry as well."

Tag picked up the letter and read the lovely bold script, a smile threatening to break out on his face. This was his chance to observe Minnie. Make sure she kept their secret. If she'd penned the letter, she planned to attend the intimate dinner at their aunt's home. "I can go with you. Keep an eye out for her sisters or cousins who attend while you calm your bride."

Jack coughed. "Now I really am worried about you. You hate public functions."

Tag stared back, attempting to look bored. "It's a family function, first of all. And I just offered my help to my oldest ally. How could I refuse this opportunity?"

"You're a good friend." Jack rose and came around the desk, slapping Tag's back. "Thank you."

Tag gave a single jerk of his chin in acceptance. He'd committed a great many shady dealings in his day, but somehow, this one made his stomach turn. He did want to protect Minnie, but he also wanted to teach her a good lesson on how she should treat a duke.

CHAPTER TWO

MINNIE STOOD in the entry with Emily gripping her arm. Not only was her cousin digging marks into her skin but she was wrinkling her sleeve's cuff. And Minnie loved this dress with its bright emerald silk and lace trim.

"Jack wrote you to confirm his attendance?" Emily asked, leaning close to her ear. She sounded near breathless.

Minnie looked up to the ceiling praying for some modicum of patience. She should have sent Diana or even Grace out with Emily. If only her parents weren't forcing her to find a husband. "For the sixth time, Emily, he's coming."

Emily's fingers dug in tighter. "Don't be cross. You know that's how this all started. He lied about where he was so that he didn't have to attend a ball with me."

Minnie sighed. "I know. I was there. And he's explained why he wasn't able to come all those times. Why he claimed to be in the country. He was engaged in a business that secured your futures." Minnie didn't like his behavior either. If that had been her fiancé she would have tossed him to the side without a glance back. He was a bad egg in her estimation along with his entire lot of friends. Especially that Duke. She rolled her eyes. The Duke of Darlington was his formal address but his friends had given him the nick-name of Daring... The Duke of Daring. Ridiculous. She gave a small snort and one of her second cousins glared at her. She quickly cleared her throat. He was a grown man running around with a pretend name and operating an illicit club. A duke at that. She wrinkled her nose as they stood. He was supposed to be a guardian for the entire country.

Just outside, carriage wheels sounded on the gravel, the crunching noise punctuated by the beat of the horses' hooves.

"He's here," Emily exclaimed finally letting go of Minnie's arm.

Minnie shook her hand, pushing blood back

down to her fingers. The door swung open and Jack stepped inside.

Instantly, Emily changed. All her worry vanished as a wide smile spread across her lips. Her body straightened and her neck lengthened. "Jack."

He crossed the foyer, reaching for her hands. "I'm so glad you sent me a missive today. This is exactly what we need."

"I'm glad you came. I…" Emily stopped stepping closer. "I'm scared."

Jack leaned in so his nose was just an inch from Emily's. "Don't be, love. I'm not going to let anything happen to you."

Emily's grin broadened but Minnie's shoulders sank. Somehow watching the couple made her ache just a little. She still didn't like Jack or agree with what he'd done but…the couple's bond was undeniable. Would she ever experience love? She'd thought she did once not very long ago. In fact, she'd nearly been engaged to a man she'd considered perfect until he'd ended their relationship. "Are we ready to go?"

Jack stepped back, tucking Emily's hand into his elbow. "Of course." He started for the door and Minnie fell in line behind them. Then he stopped and turned back toward her. "Minnie." He smiled but it didn't quite reach his eyes. "I should warn you that I've brought another guest."

She stalled, scrunching her brows. "Another guest? Who would you..." But her voice tapered off because she knew it had to be one of his friends and which one would Jack feel the need to warn her about? "Daring."

His smile vanished and his lips pressed together. "Yes. Daring."

Even as irritation made her straighten her spine, something sizzled just under her skin. "Why?" she asked, her eyes crinkling at the corners.

"I wasn't sure how many of you ladies were attending. I wanted another man to—"

"You mean rogue. Another rogue to what? Nearly ruin another Chase woman?"

Emily gasped, "Minnie."

"What? He did...nearly ruin you, that is." Minnie's hands were on her hips. "It's why you're so frightened."

Jack straightened up. "Lord Darlington will behave as a gentleman should."

"Pish." She waved. "He's no more a gentleman than you are. But let's go already. Fortunately for you, I am perfectly capable of handling such a cad and my aunt will ensure that he behaves if I can't."

Jack snapped his mouth closed without response and strode toward the door. But Emily was less inclined to let Minnie's comments go. "Don't be rude. Jack is not a rogue and neither is Lord Darlington."

Minnie clicked her tongue. "Of course they are. And why are you calling him Darlington anyhow? His preferred name is Daring. Which only underscores how much he prefers being a rogue to a gentleman."

"Minnie is right. We're not the most respectable of men," Jack said over his shoulder. Was he attempting to support her? She didn't need it.

"Well, you should be. Respectable that is. You're part of the peerage." They reached the carriage and the door snapped open. "You're supposed to be leading this country by action and example. You do neither." Minnie knew she was taking a great deal of her irritation at Darlington out on Jack. But the one time she'd met the duke, he'd been so pompous. She itched to knock him down off his high pedestal.

Jack handed Emily in and then reached for her hand as well. She stepped up into the carriage and gasped, nearly toppling back as her eyes met the dark, penetrating gaze of a hulking man curled into his seat like a waiting predator. Daring was in the vehicle. "You," she hissed as she took her seat next to Emily.

"Me," he answered as Jack climbed in. "You didn't warn her, Jack?"

"I did," Jack answered.

"You said he was joining us this evening, not that he was in the carriage. I thought a duke would take his own coach and six."

"It's wonderful to see you again, Minnie." He gave her a one-sided grin as he assessed her top to bottom.

Her insides shivered. Surely, he'd used her given name to try and intimidate her. She'd show him. "You too, Darling." She stared back. She'd called him Darling at their first meeting and he'd positively hated it. It made her heart sing. She already had a ready weapon to use against him.

"I told you the last time we met. It's Daring if you want to be impish in private, otherwise it's Darlington. I am not your darling."

"You're everyone's darling." She sat back in her chair, enjoying his irritation and considering how to strike next. "Look at that face. Angelic." She studied her gloves as she allowed her words to sink in. It wasn't that he was bad looking. In fact, he was quite handsome but not in a pretty way. His looks were harder, harsher, very masculine in fact. He had dark, penetrating, near-black eyes and strong cheekbones with a slightly hooked nose, which might have looked unattractive on another man, but with his square jaw and full lips somehow created an overall pleasing affect. The sort that made a girl's inside flutter if she weren't careful.

"Very funny," he rumbled. Then he leaned forward. "You know what you need, Miss Chase? A good lesson on what it means to be respectful."

"Tag," Jack bit out, grasping Darlington's shoulder.

"Tag?" Minnie's eyes rose from her gloves to stare into his dark glare. He'd made fun of her nickname, Minnie, all the while his name was Tag? "That can't be your given name?"

"It's a nickname," he answered, his voice dropping low.

"So your nickname is Tag Daring?" Minnie covered her mouth with her hand, a giggle escaping around her fingers. She dropped it again. This was going to be fun. "You sound like a fictional character. Like, like a spy, or a detective, or perhaps a pirate." Then she bounced a little in her seat, her brain creating several fictions all at once. "My goodness. I could write a series of books with a name like that."

His eyes narrowed. "Part of owning the club under a secret identity is having a fiction about your persona. What's wrong with that?"

"Nothing if you're eight years old." She nibbled on her lip, enjoying this moment a great deal. Never in her life had she met a man she wanted to irritate more. "Your fatal flaw as a character would be that you're actually a bit desperate for attention. I mean that name is working so hard."

"Woman," he growled.

Victory sang in her blood. Clearly she'd found a soft spot in his armor. "Man," she bit back. "My darling, Tag."

"Minnie," Emily chastised, snapping her fan against her hand. "Stop teasing him."

"I don't need your help, Lady Emily," Darlington barked, his temper visibly rising as he shifted in his seat. Rather than deter her, his emotion only fueled her to continue.

Jack knocked Darlington on the shoulder. "Mind your tone."

Darlington glared at her again. "It's her fault."

"It's her fault," Minnie mimicked his deep voice rather enjoying herself. They'd met one time for five minutes and yet he thought he could glare at her and tell her what to do. So what if he was handsome and a duke? He was not her lord and master.

———

TAG STARED across the carriage at the witch of a woman giving him an impish smile as she mimicked his voice. Bloody hell, she needed a spanking. A good old fashioned over-his-knee, skirts-pulled-up spanking.

She deserved it, he rationalized.

The image of her over his knee rose in his thoughts, her skirt pulled about her waist, her little cries of... Christ. Blood pooled in his manhood. He had to stop this. She annoyed him to the point of absolute absurdity. But if he lay his hands on her, Exile was sure to fulfill his promise of escorting Tag down the aisle. They'd agreed to watch the women, but not compromise them unless they'd a mind for marriage.

Drawing in a deep breath, he tried to calm his racing pulse. The woman got under his skin. "Apologies, Miss Chase. It isn't your fault, rather it's mine."

"That's the most insightful thing you've uttered since I stepped in this carriage," she said giving him a sweet smile that belied her words and tone.

So she didn't want to make nice? Fine. "And you've said nothing insightful, interesting, or even intelligent in either of our meetings so that means I'm a point ahead of you."

She straightened. "We're keeping score? I do like a good competition." Then she turned to Jack and Emily. "You two can be the judges. At the end of the night, you must declare a winner."

"No," Jack cut in, moving to the edge of his seat. "Don't be ridiculous."

"He's right. I can't let you tear apart Jack's friend." Emily reached for Minnie's arm.

"Wait." Tag slapped his thigh with his hand. "You think she'll win? There's no way."

"Oh please." Jack shot him an incredulous look. "She's talking circles around you."

Now he really wanted to spank her. His fingers itched as he dug them into his thigh. "I'm a bloody duke. A thousand men look to me for—"

Minnie cut him off with a laugh. "A thousand men look to a gaming hell owner who runs around calling himself Tag Daring. Lord help England. She needs it with men like you in charge."

His vision actually blurred as her other hand dug into his leg. This had been a colossal mistake. Tomorrow, he'd have to switch to babysitting a different Chase woman. There was no way he could keep his temper. He wouldn't make it through the evening without teaching Minnie Chase the lesson she so richly deserved.

CHAPTER THREE

MINNIE NEARLY SIGHED WITH RELIEF, or disappointment, she wasn't entirely certain, when the carriage arrived at her aunt's home. Darlington, or Daring, or Tag—she hadn't decided which name she wanted to call him yet—had gone completely silent after she'd insulted his ability to lead England. She supposed that may have been a bit harsh and she nibbled her lip as she gave him a sideways glance.

The man annoyed her on a level that nearly left her breathless. She'd never wanted to wound a man more and her heart pounded in her chest at the thought of sparring with him. Was that normal?

She'd never met a man who irritated or excited her as much as he did. Minnie shook her head, it didn't matter. After tonight, she'd take great pains to make sure they never saw one another again.

The door to the carriage snapped open and Darlington climbed out, Jack exited just behind him. He helped Emily out and, only after they moved away, did she realize that Darlington would escort her inside. She paused halfway out the door, staring down at him.

Slowly he held out his hand, his mouth twisting into a devilish grin. "Take my hand, Miss Chase. I don't bite."

"Are you speaking as Lord Darlington or Tag Daring?" she asked.

He gave her a tiny jerk and she wobbled on the step, her breath catching. The cad had done that on purpose. His hand came out to steady her waist and then her pulse rioted in her veins. His hand was warm and strong in a way that no man's had ever been before. Not even Lord Charleston. In fact, everything about her only serious suitor had been comfortable and easy right up until she'd met his mother.

Darlington leaned over so that his lips were near her ear, his warm breath blowing across her lobe. "You've promised to guard my secret, remember? You can't say those things in public."

Minnie swallowed. When it came to verbal banter, she was confident in her ability to best him. But here, crouched down as she exited the carriage, he was absolutely in charge. Still, her stomach fluttered with a breathless excitement at the idea. "Apologies, Your Grace," her voice came out breathy as she said the words and as he guided her the rest of the way down the step, his large hand holding tight to her middle.

"Minnie, are you all right?" Emily called from up ahead.

"Fine," Minnie answered for once with a single word, unable to explain what had just happened. Her mind was rather blank, still focused on the feel of his hand.

"Miss Chase tripped coming out of the carriage, Lady Emily, but I've seen to her safety." Darlington called, his sly grin returning.

"I didn't fall, you cad. You pulled me." But she spoke softly so only he could hear.

He coughed, clearly covering a laugh. "I don't know what you're talking about."

She tsked, knowing more words wouldn't get him to admit what he'd done. Instead they walked in silence, which might have been a mistake. Without sharp barbs between them, she became aware of how large he was, tall and muscular with broad shoulders and narrow hips that brushed hers as they moved.

She flexed her fingers on the hard ridge of his

biceps, wondering what sort of activity he did to foster such strength. She supposed all his time wasn't spent in leisurely pursuits. Were all his muscles so developed? What would he look like without his jacket and shirt?

She nibbled at her lip again, thinking of him without his clothes. Without intending to, she moved her fingers up the muscle of his arm, exploring the hard flesh.

He looked over at her, one of his eyebrows quirking. "Careful, Miss Chase. The way you're touching me, someone might mistakenly think you like me."

Her cheeks flared with heat. He'd completely caught her. "I don't have to like you to appreciate that you are a finely built man."

He chuckled even deeper, the sound running over her skin causing goose pimples to raise on the bare flesh of her arms. "I suppose you don't. In fact, sometimes that can make things quite interesting."

She slipped as her foot caught a loose stone on the path to the front door and she nearly tripped again. He steadied her once more, flattening his hand on her stomach to keep her from falling forward. "Miss Chase," he said close to her ear once again. "Are you quite all right? You seem out of sorts."

It was on the tip of her tongue to ask what things he referred to but she held her words. Instead she raised her chin higher. "I am disconcerted by being in the company of such a rogue."

He removed his hand from her stomach, sliding his fingers across the bones of her corset. "Fair enough."

She pressed her lips together to keep from gasping. He was doing this on purpose to rile her. It was working.

They climbed the steps and the door swung open, the sound of voices filtering out to them. Candles lit the interior of the foyer, giving it a warm glow. Darlington led her inside, stepping onto the marble floor. People milled on the balcony of the second floor near the entrance of the dining room.

"Minnie," her mother's familiar voice called from above.

She froze. Of course her mother was here. How had she not realized that her mother would be at her sister-in-law's dinner party? Drat.

"Minnie, dear, is that you?"

Nearly everyone stopped speaking as they turned to look at her. Her cheeks flamed hotter. "Yes, Mother," she replied weakly. No one should have heard her soft voice but the echo of the marble seemed to make it travel. Her mother, Mrs. Evelyn Chase, started down the stairs, beaming with a smile. No one had been more disappointed that Lord Charleston hadn't offered than her mother. Except for herself, of course. "Dear, are you being escorted by the Duke of Darlington?"

No. No. No. Her mother could not get any ideas about matching Minnie with the duke. She knew her mother desperately wanted her to find a husband but Darlington was the last man she'd marry. Charleston had taught her what a good match looked like and Darlington was not that man. She looked at Darlington, her face surely displaying her horror.

"Why yes, she is." Darlington gave a stiff bow, but Minnie caught the sparkle in his eye. He was going to encourage her mother just to torture Minnie. Irritation prickled all along her skin. "I'm a good friend of Lord Effington's."

"Of course. So lovely of you to join us." Her mother floated over to them, all of the assembled guests watching the show they were now putting on. "You didn't bring your sister tonight? And where is your companion?"

Dear lord in heaven, Minnie shrank into Darlington's side. Please Lord, make her mother behave. And by that, Minnie could only pray that she didn't completely embarrass her by suggesting the duke offer for Minnie's hand. "Ada was out with Emily last night. She's tired. And I didn't need a companion. Emily and Jack are my escorts for the evening, not His Grace."

"Pish," her mother said as she waved her hand. "Your Grace, we're honored to have you as a guest." She dipped into a deep curtesy.

"I'm honored to be here."

Minnie closed her eyes. This couldn't be happening. She knew why her mother looked so joyful. She was dreaming of her daughter being matched with a duke. How did she tell her mother that hell would freeze over first?

———

TAG HAD all he could do not to laugh out loud though a small snort of amusement escaped. Minnie looked like a worm squirming on a hook. He realized what was happening. Her mother was having visions of matching her daughter to him. She wasn't the first mother who'd tried and she certainly wouldn't be the last.

In this case, however, he had reason to play along. If Mrs. Chase thought there was an opportunity for a match, he'd get more invitations. Just a week or two should do it. Then, he could catch Minnie alone and have a nice chat with her about discretion. He already knew she wasn't the sort of woman to idly gossip or allow their secret to slip out of sheer silliness. Now, he was concerned she might let it fly out of annoyance, but he'd begun to formulate an argument to convince her that was a terrible idea.

She clearly didn't think much of him as a lord but still. Daring had made a promise to watch over her. If during that time, he made a compelling case to keep his secret, all the better. If being an upstanding lord was important to her than perhaps he could argue that it was the people who depended on him that would suffer if Minnie should share.

He smiled, rather pleased with what he'd already managed to discover.

"We've a small gathering on Saturday to celebrate Lord Effington and Lady Emily. You should attend, Your Grace. We'd be honored to have you."

He heard Minnie suck in a breath. He had to press his mouth together so that he didn't bark out a laugh at her expense. "Most gracious. I'd be delighted."

"No," Minnie whispered under her breath.

He heard her anyhow.

Mrs. Chase's fan fluttered toward her face. "Oh,

how wonderful." Then she turned. "Please allow me to introduce you to the rest of our family."

"No," Minnie said again, louder. "Mother. Don't overwhelm him. Please."

He knew what she meant. Don't make a big deal out of this. Somehow, this was exceedingly amusing. Most ladies of society were eager to parade him around like a strutting peacock. "I'm not overwhelmed. On the contrary, I'd be honored to meet your family."

Minnie made a choking noise next to him. He reached his arm behind her and thumped her on the back. Then he leaned down. "Don't die now, it's just getting interesting."

"I hate you," she whispered back.

An ear-to-ear grin must surely be splitting his face, but he couldn't help it. He hadn't had this much fun in ages. After having lost so soundly to her in the carriage, winning was exceptionally fun. And honestly, it was refreshing to be with a woman who wasn't trying to catch him in the marriage noose. But that made his smile slip, just a bit. When had sparring with a woman become so entertaining? And what if this was her plan? Pretend to hate him to draw him in? Women had gone through some elaborate measures to trap him. None had come close since his former fiancée. "Really? I'm quite fond of you."

"Liar," she replied as they approached an older couple. "My aunt and uncle. Look lively."

Forty-five minutes later, they'd completed the circuit. Tag might have admitted defeat, her family was a bit overwhelming. The only thing that kept him going was that she'd nearly melted into his side in her utter embarrassment. Her face was a bright shade of pink and she mumbled most of time.

Her mother had spent the entire time dropping not so subtle hints about a match between them. She spun back to them, having completed the final introduction to Minnie's great-aunt Edna. "That was exceedingly pleasant," her mother gushed.

"Says who?" Minnie muttered, her mother not hearing at all.

"I know I told you that you had this season to find a husband. I should have known that you'd deliver the best possible results."

"Mother!" Minnie's face turned as bright red as her hair. "Stop at once, I insist." She Ladymade her charmingly pink cheeks stand out all the more. "I can assure you, Your Grace, that I do not expect you to offer to court me in any fashion."

Her mother waved her fan again. "Don't be silly,

Minnie. Of course he'll court you. He just met your entire family."

The smile he'd been walking about with died on his lips. "Mrs. Chase." He raised his free hand. "Please understand that I've only just met your daughter."

Mrs. Chase leaned over and patted his arm. "Yes, yes. I know." Then she gave him a not-so-subtle wink. "But a mother has intuition about these sorts of things." Then as quickly as Mrs. Chase had arrived, she flounced off.

"What have you done?" Minnie croaked.

"What have I done?" he hissed back. "All I did was climb into a carriage with my friend."

She shook her head wildly. "You encouraged her." Then she pulled out her own fan and swatted his arm with it. "I'll be hearing about this for the rest of my life. Do you hear me?"

He cocked his head to the side. "That might make it worth it then."

"Don't be ridiculous. I'll never live it down that I allowed a duke to get away. Never mind that I didn't have him to begin with."

He raised a brow. "I see your point. And what's this about you marrying?" These were the sorts of nuggets he'd come to discover. Little tools he could use in his campaign to keep her quiet.

She shook her head. "Ada needs to have a season so I must marry or take myself off the market, so to speak. Since my parents can't stand the thought of that, they've threatened to choose a husband for me. When I lose you as a perspective suitor they're going to be so crushed, they'll surely choose someone dreadful."

His brows drew together. "Just because one potential match didn't work out?"

Minnie shook her head. "You don't understand. You're not the first man that..." She swallowed, her mouth pressing into a thin line. "I was very nearly engaged last year and—" Her face spasmed in pain. "My mother is very invested in me making a good match."

His insides twisted. While he liked sparring with her, he realized he didn't enjoy actually causing her real distress. Nor did he relish the idea of his charade forcing an unwanted match for Minnie. In fact, he found he didn't like hurting her at all. He'd come here, not just to protect her but to find any means necessary to keep her quiet. But how was he going to utilize them if he was worried about her feelings? "I appreciate your dilemma but I've my own issue to unravel. Some lovely ladies have learned a very delicate secret about me and my friends. We're attempting to make sure they do not decide to share that information."

She quirked a brow at him. "If you want to keep me quiet, you'd best leave my mother out of it."

What exactly was she saying? Was she threatening him?

CHAPTER FOUR

Tag sat at his desk the next morning ignoring the view of the rain-soaked garden beyond the windows. Instead he focused on his four friends who sat across from him. "So, as you can see, I can no longer keep watch on Minnie. One of you will have to trade with me."

Four sets of eyes stared back.

Exile was the first to speak and he shifted in his chair, clearing his large throat with a deep rumble. "I'm afraid I don't understand. You've gotten an invitation to another party. You've collected valuable information to state your case and make sure she keeps our secret. We should all be so lucky."

He let out a short breath of irritation. "Except that her family has expectations. I don't want to further those—"

"Who cares," Malice said and then gave a short laugh, his craggy features crinkling with the gesture. "We're concerned about maintaining our club's reputation and revenue stream. What happens to one girl isn't our concern."

Tag frowned. In theory Malice was right. But somehow, he did care. "But one of you could finish what I started and she need not suffer at all. More importantly, she vaguely threatened that she would tell if I didn't leave her family be."

Vice gave him the sweet smile of a man who always got his way. Why wouldn't he? With blond hair and blue eyes, people always thought him pure, when in reality, he was anything but. "She's one woman. Handle her, Daring. Besides, I've already secured an invitation to the sort of party I loathe going to so that I might accidentally run into Miss Ada. I'm not switching now."

Malice shrugged. "I've already told everyone my agenda. And I've also secured an invitation to meet my chosen lady. I'm looking for a certain type of wife and Minnie Chase does not fit the bill. Cordelia, however, just might."

Tag grimaced. He couldn't argue there. Malice wanted a quiet, unassuming woman he could marry and tuck away in his country estate. That was not Minnie. "I understand that."

Exile rubbed his neck. "Sorry, my friend, but I've got my own reasons for choosing Diana over the other girls."

"Yes," Bad rumbled, his dark features perpetually hidden in shadow. "You've already fallen in love."

Without a word, Exile used a meaty fist to knock Bad in the shoulder, nearly sending the man's chair over. It had to hurt like hell, but Bad barely made a sound.

Tag turned to him. "And you? Will you switch with me?"

Bad shook his head slowly. "The one I'm paired with, Lady Grace, is a far easier mark than Minnie. I've no appetite to make my job harder."

Well, that was a friend for you. "Your dedication to me is touching."

Bad raised a single brow. "You picked her, now she's your problem."

He pushed back from his chair and crossed to the window but he didn't really look outside. Instead, he pressed the heels of his hands into his eyes. "Perhaps we need not do this at all. They said they'd keep our secret. And they're ladies of society. Lords sniffing about is bound to cause trouble. It might be better to just leave them be."

Bad cleared his throat. "Don't you go getting soft-hearted. Remember three years ago when your farmlands flooded? You used the club's money to keep your people fed."

Tag dropped his hands. "I don't need the club anymore. My lands support themselves these days."

But Vice rose and crossed to him. "And when you finally marry and have more than one son, what will you buy with the club's proceeds? I'll tell you what. You'll have an inheritance for each of your children."

Well that was a bloody good point. "Minnie said that our club nicknames made us sound like eight-year-old boys not grown men who were supposed to lead the country."

"Viper." Malice kicked back in his chair and propped his feet on Darlington's desk. "I can hear in your voice that you're softening toward her. Worried about her future and her family. Stop. This is a job for the club's sake. What's gotten into you? It's not like you to be so mushy."

He didn't reply. He understood Malice's point, but somehow, he was beginning to see Minnie's too. "Have you ever witnessed a marriage where the two parties don't like each other?" Or in the case of his parents, hated one another.

The room was silent as the other men looked anywhere but at him.

"I don't particularly like Minnie but she does have a spirit that can be infuriating and occasionally refreshing. Depending on whom she marries, she may very well be broken. Some men don't appreciate such a strong will from a woman." He gripped the edge of his desk. His father hadn't.

Exile shifted in his chair, the legs scraping the hardwood floor. "I said this the last time we met and I'll say it again. You could just marry her. She'll keep your secret then for certain."

He shook his head. "I can't. Honestly, she reminds me too much of the first woman I nearly married." In this case, he meant the first woman he'd ever loved and the first woman to tear that affection into a thousand tiny pieces.

Vice let out a long breath. "That makes far more sense as to why you wouldn't want her. Because otherwise, I was thinking a woman like Minnie would be perfect for you."

He turned away from the window, glaring at his friend. "What the bloody hell does that mean?"

Vice shrugged. "You like a challenge. Always have. From games to women, you prefer a spirited match over the safe bet."

"It's too bad that the Countess of Abernath got to you first," Bad added scrubbing his jaw.

"She wasn't the countess back then, she was just Lady Cristina Hathaway." His hands clenched at his sides.

"Either way the countess is a she-devil." Malice said behind him. "If you ask me, you shouldn't let a woman like that ruin your future."

Tag frowned as he stared out the window. He wasn't entirely certain he had a choice.

———

MINNIE AND ADA walked along the atrium path with their arms linked. Rain pattered on the roof as leaves brushed at their skirts. "I'm sorry I didn't come to Auntie's with you last night. The Duke of Darlington really stayed by your side all evening?"

"It's all right and yes he did," Minnie sighed. "But I'm afraid I must find another suitor quickly. He doesn't like me at all so I have no idea why he spent the whole night with me other than to torture me. Once mother realizes the duke isn't actually pursuing me, I'm not going to escape her notice." That was an understatement. Her mother was going to parade her in front of every eligible lord until one showed the slightest bit of interest.

Ada winced. "I'm sure I can wait another season to come out so that you can have more time."

Minnie squeezed her sister's arm. Ada was a bit timid, but a sweeter soul had never been born. "That's so kind of you but you don't need to give up your chance for me, Ada. I've had three seasons already. I should have found a match by now." Her mouth twisted into a frown. "I just can't seem to help myself. My opinions come flying out when I really should keep them in. Men don't like it, or if they do, their mothers seem to resent me all the more."

Ada looked over at her sister. "I don't care what anyone else says, that's one of the things I like best about you. And Lord Charleston doesn't know what he's missing. He should never have ended your courtship, you were perfect for him."

Minnie inwardly winced. She'd thought them well-suited too. He'd been so easy to spend time with and that had bloomed into a great deal of affection. Perhaps not love, but Minnie had been certain the emotion would grow in time. "Thank you, Ada. I appreciate you comforting me."

"I am not just trying to make you feel better." Ada stopped walking. "You're honest and forthright. I never have to wonder where I stand."

"That's one way to look at it." But Minnie didn't consider that an actual asset. In fact, this conversation was more a reflection on how Ada was able to find the good in anyone.

"I'm serious. Some people lie, cheat, or steal. Not you. You're strong but you never use that strength to hurt anyone." Ada started walking again.

Minnie parted her lips to speak, but hesitated. She wondered what Darlington would say to that. She had a feeling he did not think of her as a kind soul.

"I'll tell you something else. The world would trample me if not for you." Ada rested her head on her sister's shoulder. "I need you, Minnie."

"Thank you," she said leaning her head on her sister's.

"Perhaps you should find a husband who needs your strength as well." Ada lifted her head suddenly. "I know that didn't work out with Charleston but surely there's another lord like him whose mother has perhaps already moved on to a less-earthly place."

Minnie pressed her lips together as she considered those words and her usually sweet sister. "Ada Lynne," she said as she gave her sister a sideways glance. It wasn't that Ada's plan was bad, and she'd considered herself fortunate to find such a good match in the easy-going Charleston. But something had shifted and a man that hid behind her skirts made her wrinkle her nose in distaste. "I'm not that difficult to get on with."

She liked a man who was strong and capable. A man whom she could spar with and who was her equal.

A man like…she didn't want to think it. Not him. A shiver of awareness rolled down her spine. Not Darlington.

"Of course you aren't." Ada quickly patted her arm. "But think on it. Men who want to be in charge often find your questions…"

"Irritating," another woman called from around the lavish shelf of orchids.

"Oh please, Diana." Minnie broke into a smile. "Like you're any better." They had both inherited the Chase personality. Strong and sharp, their fathers were brothers and apparently they had fought horribly as children. Diana and Minnie, as cousins, however, had been two peas in a pod, often understanding each other more so than any of their sisters.

Diana came around the corner, grinning. "You'll find a husband. If you don't, we'll just pick one on the street and beat him into submission."

Minnie laughed. "Not a terrible plan if all else fails."

Ada shuddered. "You wouldn't actually hit a man, would you?" Then she stopped. "Never mind. I don't want to know the answer."

Both Diana and Minnie giggled.

"Should we club a man for you too, Ada?" Diana closed the distance between them, her skirts swishing in a way that drew men to her like moths to a fire. It wasn't an act, however, it was simply how she walked.

Ada rested a finger on her chin. "I might prefer that to participating in a season, actually. I'm not looking forward to it."

Minnie gave her sister's arm a squeeze. "So when you offered to sit out for another season, you weren't just acting in my best interest?" She was teasing, of course but Ada turned a deep shade of red.

"I was speaking in both of our best interests." Ada slid her arms from Minnie's and plopped down on a nearby bench. "You can withstand mother's match-making attempts." Ada shuddered. "She's going to bully me into marrying some wretch."

Minnie took the seat next to her sister. "We're both in danger of that."

She thought again of her mother's invitation to Lord Darlington and inwardly groaned. Now she was going to have to see the intriguing man again tomorrow. "Who's with Emily?"

"Grace," Diana answered. "Why?"

"Do you think Emily would object if I didn't come to the picnic tomorrow?" The last thing she needed was another run in with Darlington. It was worth missing other prospects to avoid him.

"Only if you want her to have a complete fit." Diana squeezed next to them on the bench. "If I act like this right before my wedding, you have my permission to slap me."

"Enough with the violent threats," Ada chimed in. "If you don't want to see Darlington tomorrow, just surround yourself with other men."

"Excellent idea," Diana added. "Also, hold your tongue and snag one of them before he realizes how loud you can be."

"Your love is overwhelming," Minnie said as she rolled her eyes. But the idea had merit. She could both find other suitors and get rid of Darlington all in one day.

CHAPTER FIVE

Minnie stood behind Diana, Grace, and Cordelia, attempting to hide herself from the crowd. It was an odd position for her but she'd seen Darlington enter and she'd prefer that he couldn't find her. Ever.

She'd assumed her mother would invite a parcel of unattached males to this event but it was as though her mother had only invited Darlington, like she didn't want him to have any competition for her daughter's hand. Which might actually be true. Her mother was terribly shrewd that way.

"Do you see anyone besides him I could attach myself to?" Minnie whispered, hissing into Diana's ear.

"I'm afraid not. Oh wait. There's your third cousin, Alfred." Diana said while letting out a little giggle.

"He has had a crush on you for ages," Cordelia pointed out as she pushed up her glasses. "And he inherits the title, so mother would likely approve."

"As smart as you are, Cordelia, I don't understand why you would ever consider Alfred a viable candidate," Minnie sniffed.

"Well." Grace tossed her golden blonde curls. "I suppose if you can't find another man to deflect the duke's attention, you could send another woman to distract him. The point here is to get a match between the two of you out of your mother's head."

"I suppose that would work," she answered softly. Why did that idea upset her, causing a niggle of jealousy to twist in her stomach?

"Which one of us should it be?" Diana asked, fluffing out her skirt.

Minnie shook her head. "I don't know. He seems to hate that I'm so saucy, which would lead me to believe that Grace is the better choice, and yet he never left my side the entire dinner party. Does that mean that it should be Diana?"

Grace cocked her head. "That is strange. Though, who knows with men? They say women are too loud, too quiet, too flighty, too strong. Perhaps he just doesn't know what he likes."

Diana nodded. "So the question is would he

prefer me, who is more like Minnie, or someone more like Grace?"

"What am I?" Grace asked.

"Oh, you're all pretty and nauseatingly perfect." Diana patted her sister's arm.

"Thank you?" Grace answered.

"Isn't anyone going to suggest me?" Cordelia asked, her chin rising in the air.

Minnie pressed her lips together. Cordelia was beautiful. In fact, she and Grace were nearly identical, but it was hard to tell with her hand constantly in front of her face as she pushed up her spectacles.

"Are you going to take him on a walk and give him a tour of English garden birds?" Diana asked quirking a brow.

"That was only one time," Cordelia sniffed and all the ladies giggled.

Minnie relaxed as the light banter washed over her. Perhaps she was making a big deal over nothing. Darlington wasn't that fond of her. At the last dinner, he'd been Jack's guest. Mayhap, he'd considered it his duty to escort her. Or he'd just been punishing her for her turn

"Excuse me, ladies," a deep voice rumbled through her, making her insides quiver. "I'm hoping you can tell me where to find Miss Chase."

Grace gave him a pretty smile, perfected after

hours of staring in a looking glass. "Oh, I don't know where she is, but perhaps you'd be interested in the company of another Chase?" Grace made a slight curtsey. "I'd be happy to accompany you on a turn about the garden, Your Grace."

Minnie peeked between Diana's shoulder and Grace's fan, nibbling at her lip as they both hoped he would and would not take the offer.

Darlington quirked a brow. "Most kind of you, Lady…"

"Grace, Your Grace." Grace took a small step forward as she smoothed her skirts.

"Well Lady Grace, I appreciate the offer but I can't help but notice…isn't that Miss Chase crouching down just behind you?"

Grace gave a tiny gasp as Diana let out a huff.

Minnie inwardly groaned. Then she straightened. She was taller than either Diana or Grace and her head peeked above the top of theirs as she met the Darlington's gaze. "Must you be so persistent?"

One corner of his mouth turned up. "I must. It's lovely to see you too, Miss Chase."

He held out his hand, but she didn't take it, didn't move from behind her wall of cousins. "My mother is getting a mistaken impression on the nature of our relationship."

He raised an eyebrow. "What is the nature of our relationship?"

She straightened her shoulders even as her brow furrowed. "Do not play coy with me. We both know you have no intention of courting me. You don't even *like* me."

He held out his elbow, turning slightly to the side. "I'll try to alter the impression your mother is getting if you take a turn about the garden with me."

She gave him a long look. "How will taking a turn about the garden alter my mother's impression?"

"Humor me." He held his elbow slightly higher.

Minnie paused for a moment. What was he playing at? Should she accept? It was likely a terrible idea but she had to confess, she was curious. She gnashed her teeth. Why did she allow Darlington to pull her in when she knew she should leave him alone?

———

FOR SOME RIDICULOUS REASON, Tag held his breath. He wanted her to accept. Damn it all to bloody hell, when had he started to want Minnie's attention? Yes, he was required to seek her out, but now he was personally worried she wouldn't accept.

Slowly, she stepped forward, and threaded her

hand into the crook of his elbow. With a nod to the other women, he began walking around the perimeter of the crowd.

"Minnie?" he asked, attempting to make conversation. Now that he had her here, he wasn't entirely certain where to begin. "What's the name short for?"

"Minerva," she answered. "My mother's choice. She would never dream of using the nickname Minnie, she likes it about as much as you do."

He had to smile at that. He didn't confess that the name was growing on him. "So how did you end up with it then?"

She shrugged. "Until about three years ago, I was smaller than Ada or my cousins. They called me Minnie to tease me. Actually, first they called me Miniature but over time, it became Minnie. At the age of sixteen I suddenly grew, but by then the name had stuck." She looked over at him. "Is Tag a nickname for your given name as well?"

This one made his mouth twist as his face darkened. "It is. My mother was French and she named me Dartagnan after a French village she'd loved as a child."

Minnie's gaze was intent upon him. Did she sense there was something under the surface of this story? "She named a future English duke after a French village?"

He shook his head. Minnie was clever, which he had to be honest, he liked a great deal. But she'd honed in on a very sore spot between his parents. "She did. It made my father furious, of course. He was the fourth Duke of Darlington, all who'd been named Alfred."

"Did she do that often?" Her voice was quiet, almost soothing. "Infuriate your father?"

"Why, yes she did." He gave a shrug that was meant to be casual despite the riot in his stomach. "They'd only met a handful of times before they married, all chaperoned visits. My father once told me that she'd appeared the picture of decorum right up until the night of the wedding. He'd fallen in love with her beauty and grace, but it was not an emotion she returned."

Minnie drew in a breath, loud enough that he could hear it over the din of the party. "Oh dear. Dare I ask what happened?"

He cleared his throat. What happened was that his father's new French wife refused to share his bed. Tag was about to share when an older matron passed them, flapping her fan and giving him and Minnie a long stare, and he didn't think it suitable to continue. "I shall tell you when we know one another better."

She paused then, pulling at his elbow, which made him stop. "That is the real question of the day,

Your Grace. How well are we getting to know one another? Or maybe it isn't. Perhaps the better query is why?"

"Why?" He gave a light tug of his arm to start her moving again.

"My mother will begin inviting you to every family and social function if she thinks you are at all interested in courting me." She squeezed his arm. Her touch made him long to wrap an arm about her waist and pull her close. "Which I'm fairly certain you are not."

They were coming up on a path that went behind a raised bed of hydrangea bushes. He steered them to the right, wanting the smallest bit of privacy and sure no one would be the wiser. "And if I continue to attend the events your mother invites me to, what then?"

She gave a slight shudder. "I'd be compelled to accept your suit."

"And if I attended but never declared my courtship?" His insides twisted in guilt.

"Why would you want to do that? Why are you talking to me at all?" She stopped then. They were behind the bushes and not a soul could see them.

He pivoted around to face her, grasping her shoulder with his other hand. "Honestly, I need to know that you won't tell anyone what you've discovered about me. Which is quite a lot. The last time we spoke you threatened..."

She'd half turned to face him but stopped, blinking several times. "That's what this is about?" She gave him a push squarely in the center of his chest. "I knew you didn't want to court me. Tag Daring is a spy after all."

His lips parted as he looked down at her. "Tag was my nickname long before Daring and no one has ever put them together before. When you're not being completely churlish you're quite funny."

She huffed, pushing him again. "Glad you're amused, Tag. When you don't ask to court me, my mother is going to pair me with the first man who passes by. You'll ruin my life if you keep this up. By contrast, what is the worst that would happen if I told your secret?"

He dropped his hands, stepping away. "The club's business could dry up and—"

"You'd be forced to live exclusively off your dukedom?" Her hands came up to her hips. "Not good enough." Then she stepped closer. "Besides, I already promised I wouldn't tell anyone and I'm not going back on my word now. Please do not ruin my life over a club."

When he'd spoken with his friends, their arguments had made sense. But now, standing in front of her, they seemed thin at best and his actions sincerely as childish as she'd accused him of. "I won't ruin your life, I just need some sort of assurance that—"

She held up a finger to stop him from speaking and then slowly laid the finger against his lips. The silk of her glove brushed along his flesh and his insides tightened, a heaviness filling his limbs. "I'll make you a deal," she said quietly. "I promise to never tell a soul about the club. In return, you promise to leave me be so I can find a suitable husband as my mother has requested."

He reached up and gently wrapped his fingers about her wrist, pulling her hand away. "And how shall we seal this pact?"

She swallowed and ever so slowly, moved forward. Her movements were so subtle that he was hypnotized by them. He remained rooted as she drifted closer. "We'll seal it by giving you additional ammunition against me so that you understand just how serious I am about our deal."

Her chest brushed his and every muscle in his body clenched as she slowly rose up on tiptoe. She was tall for a woman but he was well over six feet and he reached his hand down to steady her waist, his head leaning down to meet hers.

Tentatively, she placed her lips against his. A

small brush, nothing more, but a tingling shot down his body, instantly hardening his manhood.

"Minnie," he rumbled deep and low, his need filling the one word.

She took a quick step back. "There. It's done." Her tongue darted out to lick her lips even as her head turned to the side so that she no longer looked at him.

He hooked a finger under her chin, his thumb gently guiding her face back toward his. "Is it done? Or has it just begun?"

CHAPTER SIX

Minnie stared up into the dark, dangerous pools of his eyes and her lips parted. My lord, she wanted to kiss him again. She ached with the need. Of course, she'd kissed him the first time partially because it strengthened his case, which in turn, might make him comfortable enough to leave her be. But also because she was curious. So very curious about how he tasted and how his mouth would feel.

The answer to both was delicious. He had a masculine flavor, laced with cigar and mint.

"What do you mean, we've only just begun?" Her breath came out in short gasps and they punctuated the sentence.

"Our bargain. It has just started," he said, but his gaze was on her lips.

Her heart hammered in her chest as her hands shook. Minnie took a step back. "I suppose it has."

He trailed his fingers from her chin down the column of her neck before Tag finally dropped his hand. "And you'll tell no one."

His fingers on her neck made her skin shiver in excitement and when he pulled them back, she had the urge to hunch over in loss. She forced her shoulders to stay straight. "I'll tell no one."

He nodded and then held out his elbow once again. As Minnie slid her hand into the crook, she noted how her body relaxed as she touched him. Why was that? She understood why the kiss had made her heart beat faster. She was attracted to him. Though honestly, what girl wouldn't be?

But why did she find comfort in touching Tag? She didn't understand. Her affection with Lord Charleston had been built by a mutual understanding of complementary personalities.

She and Tag finished their circle about the hydrangeas in silence and looped their way back into the crowd, no one seeming the wiser. She scanned the group again and caught a woman with pale blonde hair looking at the two of them. Minnie sucked in her breath. But the woman turned away without incident and Minnie let out her breath. "If you'll just return me to my cousins, you're free to leave whenever you'd like. In fact, the shorter your stay, the easier managing my mother will be."

He stepped around one of her great aunts and continued through the crowd. "You are in a rush to get rid of me, aren't you?" She thought she heard a pang of disappointment in his voice but that couldn't be true, could it?

The truth was, she wasn't at all. "I have to confess, you're not as bad as I first imagined—"

"High praise indeed." He grinned over at her.

A smile played at her own lips. My, but he was handsome with his face so relaxed. "But it's not you I'm concerned about."

"Your Grace, you came," her mother called from behind them.

Minnie let out a loud groan. "Do you see what we have to deal with now? She's seen us. I'll never be able to convince her that you're not a suitor for my hand."

He stopped, shifting around to face Minnie's mother. "Mrs. Chase." He straightened his elbow so that Minnie slid her fingers from his arm. He held in a grimace of dissatisfaction. When had he started to enjoy her touch so much? "I wish I could stay and chat but I've another engagement to attend."

Minnie's mother stopped short, her face falling. "Oh, that's too bad." Her gaze darted to her daughter, her brow furrowing and her mouth pinching. "Was it something my daughter said? She can be so—"

"Mother," Minnie pleaded. "Please don't."

Darlington pressed his lips together, trying not to smile, but Minnie still saw the corners of his mouth pull up.

"It was nothing that Miss Chase said," he replied. "I came today to support my friend, Lord Effington, the same reason I went to the dinner the other night." He stepped away. "But thank you for your hospitality. Most appreciated."

Her mother's shoulders drooped. "Oh. Of course, Your Grace."

Darlington might find this entertaining, but Minnie was humiliated. She closed her eyes, her head hanging low. Her mother was sure to be plotting a long lecture of feminine decorum. Which would only be more vehement if she didn't straighten her spine. Opening her eyes, she looked at Tag. "Thank you, Your Grace, for the lovely walk. Best of luck in the future."

His smile disappeared. "And you as well."

She took another step toward her mother, clamping her lips together so the bottom one didn't wobble. After that kiss, when he walked away, she might take herself to a corner and cry. "Goodbye," she said softly, her eyes on the pebble path they stood upon. They itched at the corners. What a ninny she was. She didn't actually want to cry, did she?

"Miss Chase," he said, his voice so deep that her very core shook.

Her breath caught. "Yes?" She lifted her gaze to his, somehow not able to let the air out of her chest.

"I..."

"Auntie," Cordelia cried, her feet shuffling along the gravel, the noise in stark contrast to the light pattern of people's normal shuffling. Minnie tore her gaze away from Tag to watch her cousin as she nearly sprinted toward them her chest heaving. "Oh, Auntie, come quick. My mother needs you."

"What the devil, child?" Minnie's mother chastised, her hands coming to her hips. "We're talking with His Grace."

Cordelia skidded to stop, nearly knocking into Minnie. "Oh Auntie," her voice dropped to a rough whisper. "I wouldn't interrupt but this is an emergency. Please come."

"Emergency?" Tag rumbled. "Is everything all right?"

"Fine, Your Grace." Cordelia waved while giving a high-pitched, near-hysterical laugh. Her hand waving wildly in the air. "Join the party. Make merry."

"Cordelia." Minnie reached for her cousin's hand. "You're a terrible liar. What's happened?"

Cordelia squeezed her fingers with one hand while pushing up her glasses with the other. "It's... it's Jack and Emily."

"You mean Lord Effington?" her mother chastised. "You children are far too familiar."

Minnie looked up at the sky for a moment, before she focused on Cordelia again. "What's wrong?"

"What's wrong is that Lord Effington," Cordelia said, emphasizing the name as she looked over at her aunt, "and Emily are gone."

"Gone?" Minnie squeaked.

"Gone?" Tag rumbled as he stared at both of them.

Cordelia let out a small huff. "That's what I said. Gone."

————

Bloody Christ, Tag swore to himself as he raked both his hands through his hair. This had better be a mistake. Perhaps the couple had just slipped into the bushes for a bit of privacy or a room upstairs. Embarrassing certainly but not detrimental. Unless... "Who else knows?"

"Just my sister and mother. And Ada of course."

He nodded. "Good. Don't tell anyone else. Let's pair off and search for them." If Jack had run away then he was leaving a giant mess to clean up. What if her parents refused to acknowledge the match now that they'd eloped? What if her sister retaliated by shouting their secret club to the world?

What if Minnie never spoke to him again, somehow blaming him for his friend's ridiculous actions? He swallowed down a lump that had risen in his throat. The thought of never seeing his spitfire again made him ache deep in the pit of his stomach. What a grey world his would be without her fire warming him.

"Good idea." Cordelia nodded eagerly. "Let's meet up with the rest of my family and we can break the property into sections."

"How do you know they're gone?" Minnie asked as they started across the party.

"No one has seen them for…" her voice dropped, "two hours at least." Then Cordelia licked her lips.

"But it doesn't make sense," Minnie said as she walked just ahead of him. He was listening, but his eyes kept dropping to her behind. It was rounded in the most perfect way. He wanted to cup both cheeks with his hands. He forced himself to concentrate as she spoke again. "Their wedding is only a month away. Why would they leave now? They only need to wait a few weeks." Minnie looked back at him, those green eyes capturing his as they sparkled in the sun.

"I haven't a clue." But a thought began to niggle through the rest. After what had happened, the couple had been on uncertain terms. Was leaving now their attempt to right their tilting ship?

But an hour of searching the property had yielded no results. Tag had quickly left to ride to Jack's. He could only hope they were there.

Knocking on Jack's door, the butler, Reeves, had answered. Surprise made the man's eyes go wide. "Your Grace. I'm surprised to see you."

"Why?" Tag asked as he crossed his arms over his chest.

The man blinked. "Lord Effington has left on a trip. I assumed you would be aware."

"I'm not," Tag answered, clenching and unclenching his fingers. "Where did my friend go?"

Reeves swallowed. "It's not my place to say."

Tag leaned against the doorframe, giving the man a hard stare. "And is it your place to clean up the mess that Lord Effington has made?"

"Your Grace," the man croaked.

Tag gave a heavy sigh. It wasn't Reeves' fault. "Reeves, please tell me that Lady Emily was with him so that I at least know she is safe."

Reeves had given an almost imperceptible nod. Tag's shoulders had drooped but he'd turned and left again, debating whether he returned home or to Lord and Lady Winthrop's house. He didn't have any definite news for them and what he did know wasn't good.

Then again, at least he could tell her parents with some definite assurances that their daughter was safe. Climbing onto his mount, he set off for the Bancroft residence.

He was going to kill Jack, he decided as pulled at the lapel of his coat. To be the bearer of such news... he groaned inwardly.

Would Minnie's family consider him to be cut from the same cloth as Jack? A stealer of daughters? Then he shook his head. He *was* cut from the same cloth. They ran a secret gaming hell together and why should he care what her family thought of him?

In fact, men like him probably eloped just to prove a point. He was assuming that's what had happened. Jack and Emily were in love.

He'd been in love once. He'd even proposed, thinking he wanted to spend the rest of his life with Lady Cristina. She was so much like Minnie, like his mother too. Strong, fiery, full of life, love, passion, and laughter. But just like his parents' marriage, his had been doomed before it could even start.

First and foremost, he'd met Cristina after attending calling hours to visit her sister, but from the start, she'd stolen his attention and he'd spent every waking moment thinking about her, trying to find ways to see her again. By all appearances, she'd felt the same.

The moment he asked her to be his wife, she'd accepted and taken him into her bed. He'd realized she wasn't a virgin then. Not that he'd cared. But soon, she began begging to move the wedding closer, worried she might be with child from their joining.

He'd relented, wanting his new bride protected. Then she'd pleaded for a spending account for the wedding. Which made sense, except he kept having to replenish the funds.

It wasn't until a few weeks later that he'd overheard two servants gossiping when he'd arrived at her home for an unexpected afternoon visit. It had been three months since Cristina had bled. They'd only been engaged for a month.

Still, he'd refused to believe that she'd betrayed him. And servants liked to gossip, often embellishing the truth. All people did. He'd rushed into the garden to find her and ask her what they had meant, sure this was a mistake. They were in love. He'd found her soon enough but she hadn't been alone. He'd found her in the arms of a lover.

He'd broken the engagement and refused to see her or even read her correspondence. To this day, he'd never heard a word of her explanation. Not that it mattered. What infuriated him most of all was that he'd nearly made the same mistake as his father. Married a strong-willed woman who used her power to make her husband miserable. He'd learned his lesson now.

Reaching the Bancroft townhouse, he dismounted and walked up the stairs. He raised his hand to knock when the door flung open. There he stood, fist in mid-air.

"Tag," Minnie hissed, several strands of hair having fallen loose from her coif. They framed her face in the softest way and he had the urge to reach out and touch one lock of that glorious hair. "They ran away to get married."

He dropped his fist. "My thoughts too."

Minnie shook her head, stepping out onto the steps and closing the door behind her. "No, I don't just think it. Emily's trunk is gone and in its place was a note. They've boarded a ship to Gretna Green."

"A ship?" Tag scrunched his brow, a deep frown creasing his face.

Minnie nodded, stepping closer, her hand resting on his chest. She'd smelled of fresh grass after a rain.

He itched to wrap his hands about her waist and pull her closer. He wanted to taste those soft sweet lips again. She dropped her voice only adding to the intimacy of their position. "Emily doesn't like long carriage rides."

He nodded, his chin dropping toward hers. Hadn't he just relived his past memories? Didn't he know how this ended? Why was he so tempted by the sweet lips of Minerva Chase?

CHAPTER SEVEN

MINNIE HELD her breath as his mouth drifted closer. This was a mistake. She needed a husband and everyone understood that Tag was not interested in the position.

If her mother walked out now and caught them kissing, there would be no stopping her match-making attempts. "I should…go inside." She didn't move. Her limbs refused to obey.

"I'll come with you. Your uncle will want to know what I've discovered."

She shook her head. "Don't. He's furious and threatening violence against Jack. The last thing we need is for him to decide you'd make an adequate scapegoat."

He coughed. "I can handle your uncle."

"Of course you can. You manage unruly men as a

hobby. It's him I'm concerned about. There'll be no saving this situation if you hurt him." She stepped back then, reason clearing her head a bit.

But he didn't let her waist go and suddenly pulled her tight to his chest. "Save what situation?"

What did he mean? "Jack and Emily being accepted back into the family? What else? I wish she'd told us why she's chosen to run away. It would be much easier to help her if I knew."

He stared down into her eyes, his fingers relaxing. "Of course." But he didn't let her go. "You're protecting Emily's future."

She nodded. "Yours too. I don't know how your club could be brought up but there's so many threads tying you to Jack and Emily, I think it best for your secret's sake you stay out of this as much as possible."

One of his hands slid up her back, to cup her face. "Thank you, Minnie."

She nodded. "Now you really need to go. I came out before you rang the bell, but if we're discovered out here…"

His mouth turned down but his hands slipped away from her and he took a step back. "Tell me if you learn anything new."

She shrugged. "I'll try. But trust me, you don't want my mother to know we correspond."

71

He gave his head a small shake. "I don't…"

Minnie wasn't certain if he was making a statement or asking a question the way his voice rose at the end. "Am I correct in assuming that you are not interested in marriage?"

He swallowed. "You are."

Regret niggled down her spine. "And in particular, not interested in me. Because I've been open about the fact that I need to wed."

"I'm…not," he said taking a backwards step down the stairs. He grimaced, his brow furrowing.

"Then why do you sound uncertain?" she asked, crossing her arms about her waist. She wished she hadn't asked. She was afraid of what his answer might be. After their kiss, or perhaps even before that, she'd stopped thinking of him as the worst sort of man and had begun to consider him rather interesting.

He shook his head. "I'm not. It's just…" And then he took another step back. This time, however, he slipped and in sickening slow motion, she watched him fall backwards, his head just missing a stone pillar. His shoulder glanced off the structure instead and he fell to the ground, his skull bouncing off the cobblestone. He curled on his side, letting out an agonizing groan.

"Oh dear," she cried racing down the steps.

Minnie dropped to the ground, reaching for his face. "Let me look," she said her breath ragged. She didn't see anything but then she slid her fingers into his hair, a lump already forming by the base of his skull.

"I'm all right," he ground out. "It's my shoulder more than anything."

Minnie looked lower to realize that his arm was at an odd angle. "Oh dear," she whispered more to herself. "Don't move."

"I couldn't if I tried," he grunted between clenched teeth.

"If they ask, I came out and found you like this," she said close to his ear. The last thing she needed was for her family to try and force a match. She was not interested in trapping a man in marriage. She was many things, but manipulative wasn't one of them.

She didn't wait for his reply as she jumped from the ground and, lifting her skirts, sprinted back up the steps. "Come quickly," she yelled as she opened the door. "I've found the Duke of Darlington injured on our drive."

Without waiting for a response, she hurried back to his side and plopped on the ground next to him to cradle his head in her lap. Smoothing back his hair, she curled her body around his. "Try not to worry.

I've got you. I'll not let anything happen to you, I swear."

"Somehow," he groaned. "I believe you."

She smiled a little at that. "You should, I'm practically holding your life in my hands."

"There's the Minnie I know and love."

"Wait," she cried, her mouth going dry and her body freezing. "Did you just tell me you love me?"

———

TAG SWORE SOFTLY under his breath as he turned his head to look up at Minnie. Pain shot down his side. He should lie and tell her that he meant affectionately, not romantically. But he wasn't certain he was capable of the lie in this moment. "You know what I meant."

She didn't answer as people began to flood out the door from the house. In fact, she didn't meet his gaze at all. He wished Minnie would tell him what she was thinking.

Her mother dashed to the front the pack. "Your Grace!" she yelled, stopping within a breath of him, her hands crossing over her heart. "Your arm."

Minnie stared up at her mother, her brows drawing together. "I'm sure he hadn't noticed until you mentioned it."

A single bark of laughter erupted from his throat and then he spasmed in pain.

Several gasps erupted around him. "Is he going to be all right, Minnie?" one female voice asked.

"Yes, Ada, but go and tell Mr. Hoffsman to fetch the doctor. Hurry." Minnie stroked his face as she cradled his head in her lap. If not for the searing pain in his arm and throbbing in his head, he might actually enjoy this. She'd curled around him, her bosom pressing against his ear.

"What should we do?" another female asked.

"He's friends with Effington, isn't he?" A gruff male voice grumbled from his right.

"He fell on our property," someone else answered.

Minnie cleared her throat. "He's been searching for Emily and came back to tell us what he'd discovered, Uncle. He's here to help." She began rhythmically stroking his hair as she crooned nonsensical words of comfort. Everyone else quieted and he closed his eyes. The whole thing was rather lovely.

"Are you with me?" She stopped stroking and her voice rose, worry making it high and tight.

"I'm here," he answered without opening his eyes. "And I'm not going anywhere." He wanted to beg her to start petting him again. He'd nearly forgot about the pain at her touch. What was happening to him?

He was going soft over Minnie Chase. He knew deep in his gut that it was a mistake, but he couldn't help himself in this moment. Not only was she attractive, breathtakingly so, but her touch was so warm, so giving and inviting. Made a man ache.

"They're on the way to fetch the doctor," Ada called.

"Good," Minnie answered. "Collect up some servants so that we can lift him without harm."

Tag relaxed more deeply into her lap. Minnie was a woman who had the situation well under control.

Funny, he'd never considered how helpful a strong partner might be. He'd only seen the downside of a woman with an iron will. "How do you think I'm going to get home?" he asked as her hand started its rhythmic movements again. He wanted to sigh with contentment.

"You're not," she replied close to his ear. "You're staying here."

"All right," he said, trusting her to know what was best. "Where will you be?"

"I'll be here too," she said even more quietly. "I'll not leave you now."

"Good," he answered. So good. He had the sudden feeling that he could stay wrapped in her arms forever.

"Lord Darlington." She continued stroking.

He frowned when she called him by his real name. He liked the way *Tag* rolled off her tongue. It shouldn't be *Lord Darlington*.

"Yes?" he asked trying to open his heavy eyelids.

"I wanted to tell you that..." She stopped and her hand stilled too. "That I like you. A great deal more than I thought I would. Despite how we met...I think you're...well...you're a good man."

He opened his eyes and shifted his head so that he might look into the emerald green of hers. "I like you too. A great deal more than I thought I would."

She smiled down at him, a brilliant grin that lit her face. "We're friends then?"

"Friends." The word left a bitter taste in his mouth. Why was the idea of being friends so dissatisfying and what could he do about it?

CHAPTER EIGHT

MINNIE STARED down at the injured man in her lap, her insides as soft as churned butter. Even with his shoulder hanging low and the sleepy expression on his face, he looked every bit the powerful man that made her heartbeat quicken. More so, with the intimacy of their position. His large chest spilled from her lap and his muscular legs stretched way out, near reaching the steps. Her family stood staring at them and yet she had the urge to lower her mouth to taste his mouth again.

She licked her lips, trying to gain control of her thoughts. But his eyes honed-in on the gesture and her insides tightened.

She was looking for a husband. She repeated that fact several times until it became a chant in her head. *Don't go all mushy, you're looking for a husband. Don't stare at his lips, you're looking for a husband.* See, he caused her brain to go soft as well, she was never this redundant.

Several servants hustled out the door and quickly lifted Tag from the ground. They managed to set him on his feet as Minnie stood too, her own legs wobbly.

He stumbled but caught himself and one of the servants positioned himself under Tag's good arm to help him into the house.

Minnie did not see Tag for the next several hours as the doctor attended him and then dinnertime began.

She excused herself early and went to her room, then readied herself for bed. Her family had discussed Emily and Jack's situation in circles for hours and she needed quiet to sift through her jumbled thoughts.

Not that she wasn't concerned for her cousin but Minnie knew in her heart that Jack and Emily had made a decision together and likely for good reason. They loved one another and must have thought this the best choice for their future.

It was her own situation that plagued her now. She liked the duke a great deal, but she had been tasked with finding a husband and she could not dwell on a man who did not want a wife like her: strong-willed and opinionated.

A knock sounded at the door. "Come in," she called, turning to see who it might be.

Her mother opened the door, gently closing it behind her. "Are you feeling all right?" she asked as she crossed the room where Minnie had been staying at her aunt and uncle's. She supposed now that Emily had run away, she should return home.

"I'm fine. Just thinking." Minnie stood and crossed to her mother, kissing her cheek.

"I've just been to visit His Grace. They've reset his shoulder and he should be fine to return home in the morning." Her mother reached for her hand and then led her toward the bed.

"Thank you for the update, Mother." She let her mother pull her along, relief making her a little weak.

"I want to discuss your relationship with him," her mother said when they reached the bed.

Minnie inwardly groaned. "Not tonight, Mother. I'm tired."

Her mother shook her head. "Today I won't remind you that you need to find a husband. That Ada has to have a season. You made it clear at the party that you weren't interested in the duke."

Minnie shrugged. Something was raw inside her

and she couldn't lie. "That isn't what I was trying to say. There is no future with the duke."

"Ah," her mother answered. "I was going to say that I can see it on your face that you like him a great deal and, honestly, he likes you too."

Minnie dropped her chin. Somehow those words didn't make her feel better. "He doesn't want to marry, Mother, and I believe, even when he does eventually choose a bride, she will not have my... colorful personality."

"What's wrong with a little personality," her mother sniffed.

That made Minnie smile, her hand stretching out to touch the back of her mother's. "You hate that I am so loud. That I talk so much and offer my opinion so freely."

Her mother shrugged, but she squeezed her daughter's fingers. "I don't hate it, dear, I dislike that it makes your life so difficult. And just to be clear, he doesn't hate it either. In fact, I think he quite likes your strength." Her mother stood. "But I trust you to interpret his intentions. If he doesn't want you as a wife, you're right to leave him be and move on."

Minnie gave a nod. She closed her eyes and pictured the duke's face as he looked up at her. The problem she supposed was that she wanted him to want her. But his only real concern was protecting his club.

Her mouth twisted down into a frown. When had her feelings gotten involved? It was that kiss.

There was nothing to do for it, she had to tell Tag that he needed to leave her be. The issue was that her mother was right, she did need to marry for Ada's sake. She should have been married already.

Lord Charleston had been about to propose. He'd been handsome and kind and she'd liked him immensely. She supposed, in retrospect, he didn't make her feel the way Tag did, but still. She'd thought Charleston a good match. He was quiet, reserved, and often soothed her rougher edges.

The problem had come when she'd met his mother, who'd taken an instant dislike to Minnie. They'd hosted mother and son for dinner and by the end of the evening, Minnie could not contain her annoyance with the constant barbs Lady Charleston had tossed her way. She'd snapped back. "I'm offensive? Have you listened to yourself?"

The result had been a hasty finish to the dinner and a carefully penned note from Lord Charleston expressing his deepest affection but his absolute regret that their relationship could go no further.

Minnie hadn't cried. But inside, she'd died a bit. She'd always known that she was too blunt for some people. His rejection had hurt her deeply. She'd gone through the last season afraid to allow any man close again. Though, she no longer had a choice. And she supposed, Tag had helped her in one regard. He'd pushed right past the defenses she'd put up with his large shoulders and his secret club.

She stood. She'd like to tell him that, actually. But she also needed to be clear. They'd made a bargain. He had to leave her be.

Grabbing her dressing gown, she pulled it on and crept from the room. Stealing from shadow to shadow, she made her way to the guest wing.

Minnie had no idea which room was his so she stationed herself in a dark corner to watch. It didn't take long before one of the doors swung open. Minnie recognized the groom who'd helped Tag into the house. "Is that all, Your Grace?"

"Yes, thank you. Tell the staff they need not return for the night," Tag's deep voice rumbled out the door.

With a nod, the groom started down the hall. Minnie watched him until he disappeared and then headed for the door.

It opened with a soft click and she slipped inside the dark interior, only firelight dancing in the grate cast light into the room.

"Really, I'm fine. I don't need—"

"Tag," she interrupted him. "It's me."

"Minnie," he said, his voice making her shiver and she turned toward the bed.

She had the urge to hold his head in her lap again and without thinking, she crossed the room and sat next to him on the bed, reaching out her hand to brush the hair back from his forehead. "Are you all right?"

"I'll be fine. Now that the shoulder's back in the socket, it already feels much better." He captured her bare fingers in his and brought them to his lips, kissing each one before he placed his mouth in the center of her palm. "Thank you for helping me today."

She swallowed, her insides tingling with every touch. "You're welcome." She gently pulled her hand from his. "I'm glad you're going to be all right."

He gave her a soft smile. "I am."

"I came here," she started, taking a deep breath, "to actually thank you."

"Why?" he asked his brow scrunching.

She shrugged. "I know that you've only been spending time with me because you were worried about your secret, but for me, this experience has helped me a great deal."

His eyebrows rose. "How so?"

She nibbled her lip. "Well. I was courted by Lord

Charleston and when it didn't work out, I thought I might not be able to trust my affection to another man again but—" She stopped, realizing that she'd inadvertently admitted that she felt affection toward Tag.

"But what, Minnie?"

———

WAS she trying to tell him that she was sweet on him?

That should have filled him with dread. Instead, a nameless excitement pulsed through his veins. "But what, Minnie?" he asked again.

"I..." Even in the dark he could see the flush of color staining her cheeks. He raised his hand and stroked his thumb along the warm flesh. "I enjoy your company."

His thumb reached her chin and began trailing down the delicate skin of her neck. "That is your big announcement? You came to my room in the dark of night, braving ruin to tell me that you enjoy my company?"

Her lips pressed together and he thought for a moment that she was angry, but then her hand came up to cover her mouth. From between her fingers came a tiny squeak and then another. She dropped her hand and a full-on laugh escaped her lips. "That is ridiculous, isn't it?"

He found himself grinning back. "A bit."

Another giggle escaped her lips and then another as a full-on laughing fit threatened to overtake her. She dropped her face to his arm, burying her laughs into the blankets. He reached over and gently stroked her hair as her laughs subsided.

"What happened with Charleston?" he asked, brushing a bit of her hair back from her face.

She sighed and lifted her head a bit. "Nothing terrible. It just didn't work out."

He gave her a gentle tug and she responded by stretching out next to him. He tried to remember the last time a woman had just lay next to him. Gathering her close to his side, he found he quite liked it. Her body fit against his in the most satisfying way. Part of him ached to run his hands over more of her, kiss her lips, but he ignored the desire. Instead he held her close. "If it wasn't so terrible then why are you thanking me?"

She sighed as she snuggled in closer. "He didn't like how brash I was. How bold. It's not that I don't understand this about myself. I try to hold it in but it comes out anyhow and…" She paused, swallowing. "I wish I could change that about me and I suppose it hurt that he didn't like it either."

The ache in his chest throbbed on her behalf. "Minnie," he started, but stopped to turn his head and softly kiss her forehead. "Some man is going to love how strong you are."

She shook her head, rubbing her cheek on the crook of his shoulder. "I don't have time to find that man. I've told you already." She rested her hand on his chest.

He closed his eyes. Part of him wanted to offer to be that man for her. Marry her, accept her for who she was. But memories of his own parents assaulted him. The way they'd constantly fought, each warring for control, often using him as a pawn in their battle. He'd thought he was different but Christina had taught him he wasn't. When he'd tried at love, he'd failed just as miserably. "My father fell in love. Both of my parents were so strong-willed, that affection turned into a battleground. Perhaps, a marriage of convenience will suit you."

"Your parents were a love match?" she asked as she lifted her head.

He nodded. "At least on my father's part. But that affection turned to hate. They fought daily, their arguments often turning violent."

She curled her fingers into his chest. "Oh, that must have been awful." She lay her head back down. "My mother can be difficult but generally speaking, she means well. She loves us, she just wants to help us in the most annoying way possible."

"Like insisting that you marry?"

She shook her head then settled into the crook of his neck. "That is for Ada's benefit and she's right. It's time I gave my sister the chance to enjoy society and find a husband of her own."

He could hear the love in her voice when she spoke of her mother and her sister. He gathered her closer as though he might glean a bit of it being next to her. "Very generous of you."

She sighed. "I wish I'd married already." Then she tapped his chest. "What do you wish?"

He wished his childhood had been different. More than that, he wished he'd never met Cristina. Maybe then his heart could be open. Open to having Minnie in his life. "I wish I hadn't backed down those steps today."

She smiled against his neck, he felt the change in her face even if he couldn't see it. "Does your shoulder hurt terribly?" She trailed her fingers up over his collarbone, lightly touching his wounded arm.

He relaxed into the touch. "It feels much better now." Tomorrow he'd leave and go home. There was no reason to see Minnie again. He ached a little thinking of their relationship drawing to a close. He looked over at her, staring at her full lips in the fire light, memories of the kiss they'd shared heating his flesh. It had been a light touch. Why had it affected him so deeply?

She pushed up to a sitting position and he missed her heat. He almost pulled her back down but his fingers curled into the blankets. That would be a mistake.

"I'm glad." She slowly stood. "Thank you again, Your Grace." She was putting space between them. Physically, of course, but emotionally too. "I'm glad to have met you."

Then she turned and left the room. He had the distinct impression that he'd made a terrible mistake in letting her go.

CHAPTER NINE

TWO DAYS LATER, Minnie stood between Cordelia and Grace watching a parade of dancers float by. She'd danced a few sets herself but was thankful to have a repose between partners.

"What did Lord Knightly ask you while you danced?" Cordelia tucked her head to the side to keep her voice from travelling. "Tell me again. It's too amusing to miss."

Minnie sighed. "He asked how I felt about Siamese cats. Apparently, he has ten of them."

"Siamese?" Grace crinkled her brow. "Aren't they the howlers?"

"Imagine living with ten howling cats?" Cordelia chuckled. "I'll have to thank Lord Knightly. He has completely distracted me from worrying about Emily. At least for a few minutes."

Minnie's mouth pinched down into a frown. They'd received no word from her cousin. Minnie thought she understood why they'd run off. They needed to marry on their terms without the interference of Jack's friends or Emily's family. But to not even send word? Something else must have happened.

They'd only come tonight to cover her absence. As far as the rest of society knew they'd have the wedding as planned.

She kept that to herself however, instead she regaled her cousins with stories about her dance partners.

"Don't even get me started on Lord Rakenburg. He insinuated I wasn't a good candidate because I had a sister and four female cousins. Apparently, I am ill-fitted to making male heirs. We can add that to my list of negative attributes."

"We have loads of male cousins." Cordelia raised a finger on one hand as she pushed her glasses up with the other.

"You don't need to convince me," Minnie answered as she looked to the ceiling. "But I think Rakenburg could use a good lecture on the proper methods of choosing a bride."

"Drat," Cordelia hissed spinning around so her back faced the crowd. "It's him."

"Who?" Minnie craned her neck, Tag's face jumping to the forefront of her thoughts.

"I don't know his actual name." Cordelia pushed up her glasses. "He was the one that caught me in that silly club. I think they called him Malice." Cordelia gave a shiver. "What sort of name is that for a man?"

Minnie nibbled on her lip, it did sound rather dark. "Darlington is Daring, that's—"

"Daring is exciting and interesting," Cordelia pressed her fingers to her cheeks. "Malice is just plain frightening."

"He was rather chivalrous. Catching you and all," Minnie said the words but she didn't feel them. She had a feeling that none of those men, save Jack, wanted to marry or live traditional lives. Even Jack had stolen her cousin away right before their wedding. Cordelia was likely right to fear Malice. "But if he makes you uncomfortable, then by all means, stay away."

"Excuse me." A beautiful woman stopped next to Minnie. "What dreadful man are you ladies staying away from?"

Minnie crinkled her brow, staring at the blonde's icy visage. Minnie knew who she was but couldn't quite place her. Something about the color of her hair was so familiar. "You're mistaken, but thank you for your concern."

Grace tucked slightly behind Minnie, her small hand resting on Minnie's shoulder, even as Cordelia spun back around.

The woman gave them an odd look. Her smile indicated she was attempting to be friendly, but there was a hardness about her eyes that was anything but. "No need to lie to me. I have met loads of men that I find loathsome or downright dangerous. We women have to stay together to keep ourselves from harm."

Then she turned and looked about the crowd. "We wouldn't be discussing the Marquess of Malicorn, would we?"

Minnie pulled her chin back. Darlington was Daring at the club and Jack, as the Earl of Effington, had been called Effing. It was possible that Malice was Malicorn. "I couldn't say, truthfully."

"Is he the one over there with the sharp features who is staring at us like a wolf watches sheep?"

Minnie glanced over at Malice. That wasn't a bad description. He was moving closer, his gaze unwavering. "Could be."

"I'll dispose of him for you. Worry not." Then she leaned in closer. "I'm having a soiree later this week. Watch for my invitation."

"Forgive me," Minnie said as she stared at the woman. "But who will the invitation be from?"

The other woman trilled a laugh. "How silly of me. I'm the Countess of Abernath. Pleased to meet you, Miss Minerva Chase."

Minnie sucked in her breath. Grace grabbed her shoulder and Cordelia took a step back. The countess had told Emily about the club to begin with. Minnie didn't know why but she was sure this woman was set upon making trouble. "Forgive me, my lady, but I don't know if we'll be able to attend."

The countess quirked a brow. "Don't be hasty. There will be a great many bachelors there. In fact, The Earl of Winston is most anxious to meet you." She gave Minnie an encouraging smile. "A fine catch for a woman like yourself."

"Why are you helping her?" Cordelia squeaked out.

Minnie frowned. She wasn't sure it was help this woman was offering. She'd nearly destroyed Emily and Jack and she was certain the Countess's actions had led to the couple eloping. Her eyes narrowed. The hair... Minnie remembered where she'd seen that distinctive shade of pale blonde. Her family's garden party, which had been the last time Emily and Jack had been seen.

"Like I said. We ladies must stick together, especially when it comes to men of ill intent." Then the countess tucked her chin, moving closer and dropping her voice. "I once knew Darlington. Stay away from him, if you value your reputation at all. He'll never offer for you, he'll only set you to ruin."

Then the woman whisked off, straight toward Malice.

She stopped in front of him, intersecting his path toward them. Minnie couldn't hear a word but she watched Malice's face change. He went from his usual dark stare to his features turning absolutely black even as he straightened away from the countess. Then, without a word, he turned and headed for the door.

The countess spun back toward them and sashayed to where they stood. "See ladies? I've taken care of that vexing problem for you."

"What did you say?" Grace squeaked out from behind Minnie.

Minnie tried not to huff at her cousin. Grace had always been delicate.

"I simply told him that I'd already warned you of his rakish tendencies and he needn't bother to approach. You wouldn't see him."

Minnie remained silent, but she doubted very much that's what the countess had said. The only person to confirm or deny that, however, would be the Marquess of Malicorn. Somehow, finding out the countess's motives would help her discover what had happened between Emily and Jack. She needed to find out what had been said and only one man could tell her where to find Malicorn. Tag…

———

TAG SAT in front of a roaring fire in his study, sipping a snifter of scotch. The burning liquid was doing little to extinguish the feeling he'd made a terrible mistake. He'd said goodbye to Minnie.

Though the words had been the same as any other parting, they'd both understood that they had no reason to see each other again.

Except, as the last two days had passed, he'd thought of a reason. He missed her. Truly and deeply he craved her company, the banter, the tension, the way wisps of her hair loosened from her coifs. He longed for the press of her lips when she was about to deliver one of her perfectly aimed barbs and the flush of her cheeks when she drew near him.

Bloody hell, he raked his fingers through his hair, setting his glass down with so much force, liquid sloshed over his hand. He'd told himself for years now that he'd never marry a woman like his mother, or like Cristina. He'd find a docile miss and mold her into the wife he wanted.

The more he thought about it, the worse that idea sounded. He watched the flames dance as he reasoned out the whys of it. First, his mother had never loved his father. Though she'd pretended at the beginning, she'd married him for his status. He'd surmised that much from the fights he'd overheard. And Cristina, he could only assume that she'd also been motivated by station and finances when she'd accepted his proposal. Why else would she have a lover while ensnaring a duke?

But that only made him grimace. Minnie hadn't been subtle. She was in the market for a husband. And that had kept him away. But there were other traits that pulled him dangerously close.

Cristina would never have cradled him in her lap the way Minnie had. In fact, neither would his mother. She'd responded to his childhood illnesses and injuries with mild distaste, or even, on a few occasions, severe displeasure. When he'd broken his arm falling from a tree at the age of eight, she'd told him that's what he got for being so foolish and then left for London for the six weeks the injury had healed.

"She's a hard woman," his father had consoled.

Minnie would never mistreat her family. She'd

protect her loved ones with everything she had. He thought of the way she'd defended Emily on the first night they'd met. The way she was marrying for Ada's sake.

And the way she'd held him while he was in bed injured. She didn't expect him to marry her but she'd wanted to touch him...hadn't she?

"Excuse me, Your Grace," the butler called from the doorway. "The Marquess of Malicorn is here to see you."

"Here...now?" He turned. What did Malice want at this time of night? "See him in."

A few minutes later, Malice strode through the door with his usual swagger about his shoulders, but his face was drawn and tense. He tossed himself into a chair next to Tag. "Well. I knew when your old lady friend cornered Emily and told her about the club, it wasn't a good sign. We should have been watching Lady Abernath instead of the Chase women."

"What's happened?" Darlington sat up straighter, dread making his legs heavy.

"I went to the party. The one I'd secured an invitation for. I mentioned it last week."

Tag rolled his hand, wanting Malice to tell the story already. "Yes. Yes. You're a marquess. Invitations are not difficult for you."

Malice raised his brows. "You're as prickly as that little chit, Minnie."

"She is Miss Chase to you," Tag snapped.

Malice sat back in his chair, his gaze piercing as his mouth thinned. "It's good that I've come."

"Why is that?" Tag sat forward, growing more impatient by the second. It was near midnight and his friend was talking but saying nothing.

Malice frowned as he tented his hands in front of his face as though he were making a profound statement. "You're sweet on her."

The words pushed him back in his chair. Was it that obvious? His heart raced in his chest as he considered his feelings. "What does Minnie have to do with you arriving here in the middle of the night?"

"I attended that ball—"

"You've said," he bit out.

"And Lady," he drew out the word, his lip curling, "Minerva was there. As was the Countess of Abernath."

"Bloody effing bullocks," Tag roared, pushing out of his chair, then pacing over to the fire. "Did they meet?" The countess was a woman who hurt people. If she hurt Minnie, he'd make her pay the way he should have years ago.

"Oh, they met." Malice sneered around the

words. "Looked chummy even. They chatted for a while. Laughed and talked."

"You…you're joking." Sick dread filled his stomach. Perhaps the countess hurting Minnie was not the problem at all. "Did they seem to know each other?"

"I couldn't say. But they talked for a long time. And then Abernath approached me with a message to you."

"A message?" Dread formed deep in his gut.

"The countess said, and I quote, *'Tell Daring that Lady Minerva is going to help me make him pay for what he's done.'*"

CHAPTER TEN

MINNIE SAT for her calling hours the next morning, tapping her chin, wondering how she was going to speak to Tag. If only Emily were here, she'd be able to help. Then again, if Emily were here, she wouldn't need to unravel this mystery.

Of course, a tiny voice whispered that she just wanted to see Tag again. But she pushed that annoying suggestion aside. This wasn't about him and the way he filled her with breathless excitement. Or the way she seemed to crave his touch.

She turned her head to stare out the window down to the street. She needed to focus on Emily. Why would she and Jack have decided to run away?

But she caught a familiar crest as a carriage rumbled to a stop in front of their town house.

She stood as Tag exited the vehicle, making for

their front stairs. She caught her breath as she stared down at his broad shoulders, his long stride carrying him quickly to the door.

Her chaperone looked up at her. Mary was an older, unmarried cousin who'd come to visit for the wedding. She referred to herself as a spinster but Minnie liked to think that Mary could still have any man she chose. At five and twenty, she was a beauty to be certain. "What is it?"

"His Grace," she said, her hand fluttering somewhere between her face and her waist. "How is my hair?"

Mary smiled. "Red."

Minnie wrinkled her nose then stuck out her tongue. "Very funny."

"By the way, a letter also came for you this morning." Mary pointed toward the secretary. "It has the Abernath crest upon it."

"You know the Abernaths?" Minnie put her thoughts of Tag aside as she crossed the room to her cousin.

"Of course." Mary frowned. "The Countess of Abernath regularly hosts large social events. During my two seasons, ladies prayed for an invitation, though mothers of eligible girls often refused them."

"Why?" Minnie leaned forward her hands clasped.

Mary bent forward as well, her voice dropping. "The rules were somehow different at the Abernaths. People were less...inhibited."

Minnie sat back. "Somehow, that makes sense."

"Do you know her? Is that an invitation to her home?" Mary's eyes widened. "Oh Minnie, don't go."

Minnie crossed the room and tore open the note. Sure enough, it was an invitation from the hostess. She dropped the note to the desk. "Of course she promised me that all sorts of eligible bachelors would be in attendance. Dangling a carrot in front of my face."

The door creaked open. "Miss Chase." Their butler stepped into the room. "The Duke of Darlington is here to see you."

"See him in." She swallowed, forgetting all about the countess or the party as she moved toward the door.

"No need," Tag's deep voice called. "I'm already here."

Her heart jumped up into her throat. "Your Grace," she said, her voice breathy and she raised a hand to her throat to calm her jittery nerves.

"Miss Chase," he replied, inclining his head as he stared at her, his back stiff and his mouth pinched into a frown.

"Is everything all right?" She took a step closer,

her voice dropping. Something was off. There was no warmth in his gaze today, the lines of his face hard. "Have you heard from Lord Effington?"

He shook his head. "I have not." He pulled at his jacket, smoothing the fabric over his massive chest. "But I did receive word from the Countess of Abernath."

That made her pause. "Did she invite you to her party too?"

"Party?" he asked, his brow furrowing.

She spun about and reached for the invitation. "Yes. I just received this." She picked up the letter and brought it to Tag.

He scanned the contents. "And I suppose you want me to come with you?"

Now she knew something was amiss. Normally, he was eager to attend social events with her, claiming it was his duty to do so. "Why would you come with me? We've already decided we shouldn't be seen together anymore. I'm not sure why you're even here."

He carefully folded the note, handing it back to her. "I'm here because of the countess's message."

Now she was truly confused. "What message?"

He tugged at his coat again, his face pulling into severe lines. "As if you don't know."

Minnie cocked her head to one side, looking at

him as she tried to discern what they were even discussing. "I met the Countess of Abernath for the first time last night and suddenly an invitation shows up at my door along with an angry duke. You're going to have to explain this to me because I am thoroughly perplexed."

He gave his head a stiff shake. "I'm not playing your game any longer, Minerva. Tell me what you and the countess are plotting."

His accusation made her angry. "You think that I am plotting something with her?" Her shoulders straightened. "She's the very woman who nearly destroyed Emily. Remember my cousin who is now missing. Are you insinuating that I had something to do with her disappearance as well?"

His face paled. Just a little. "I do remember that now. She told Emily about the club."

"She did. And she told me that you broke her heart." Minnie stepped closer. "I don't know what happened between the two of you, and honestly, it's none of my business."

His lips pressed into a hard line. "You're right. My past isn't your concern."

"But I'll not be involved in this mess by either of you." She waved the invitation in her hand. "You're free to go. I hope never to see you again."

———

TAG GRUNTED IN RESPONSE. He knew he'd made a mistake, he just wasn't sure which mistake that was. Had he falsely accused Minnie? Had he mistrusted her in the first place? Either way, he wasn't done with this conversation despite her dismissal.

"I'm not leaving so you may as well sit." He gestured toward the chair. He heard her chaperone squeak from the corner but he ignored the other woman.

She huffed. "This is my home. I'll decide when I sit and when I don't."

"Fine," he answered taking a seat. "So you're telling me that you had never met the countess before last night?"

"That's correct. Though she knew exactly who I was. Of course, Malice was staring at us with an intensity that must have all of London wagging their tongues this morning."

Tag gritted his teeth. Cristina knew exactly who his friends were and apparently she knew about the secret club he ran. He'd been seen publicly with Minnie on more than one occasion. If the countess were checking in on him, it wouldn't take much for her to learn of his interest in Minerva Chase.

Of course, part of him still wondered if Minnie

had a more active role in Cristina's plan, whatever it was. Even his own mother had used him as a weapon in her war against her husband. And he'd never been anything to Cristina other than a plan to secure her future. Why wouldn't Minnie be plotting something? "And what did she say to you?"

"She said that she'd take care of Malice for us. He makes Cordelia uncomfortable." She slid into the chair across from him, keeping her back straight. "What I wanted to know is what she said to Malice."

"Why?" he asked, sitting up. Something in this conversation wasn't squaring.

Her mouth dropped open. "Why? The Countess of Abernath is at the root of Emily and Jack's elopement. I can't prove it yet, but I'm certain it's true." She licked her lips. Despite his mistrust, he clenched in awareness. "I saw her at the garden party where they disappeared. If I'm going to figure out why they left, I need to learn more about the woman who started this entire affair."

He ran both of his hands through his hair, likely causing it to jut out at odd angles. "She told Malice that she was going to exact revenge on me."

Minnie gasped, her hands covering her mouth. Slowly she dropped them again. "Revenge on you? Why?"

Bloody hell. "We were engaged to be married."

She leaned forward, her expression pained. "Engaged?"

He shook his head, rubbing the back of his neck. "A long time ago. Yes."

"What happened?"

He'd never shared this with anyone, save Jack. And that was only after several drinks. "I found her with another man." He didn't tell her about the pregnancy or the fact that she'd likely tried to pass off another man's child as his. "But she was still furious with me. She quickly married the Earl of Abernath but..." How did he say that she hated her husband and had only married him to secure her child only to lose the baby?

"I don't need you to say more. I think I understand." Minnie slumped back down in her chair. "Do you think she told Emily about the club to punish you through Jack?"

Tag sat forward. "That is very likely and terribly clever on your part." Minnie was so smart, he couldn't help but admire her. "I've been wondering the same."

"If I am so clever, why don't I know why Emily and Jack left?"

He let out a long breath. "You just don't have all the information." Should he tell her? Away from Minnie, he'd convinced himself that she was just another woman attempting to manipulate him, but here, in this room, staring into the green of her eyes, he had a much more difficult time believing that to be true. Or perhaps, he just didn't want to believe she'd ever intentionally hurt him.

"What information?"

"Jack inherited the title and a mountain of debt. He's worked at the club to make his own holdings profitable. I only started the business as a silent partner in support of my friend."

Minnie stared at him, her mouth hanging open. "You financed the club for Jack?"

"I did. He's only recently paid my investment back and shorn up his own holdings. But he was worried he wouldn't be able to support Emily in the lifestyle she deserved without continuing to participate in the club's activities and daily operations."

She rubbed the sides of her face with the tips of her fingers. "And Emily was concerned that he didn't really love her. She was just a means to an end."

The details fell into place. "By eloping, he's given up her dowry."

Minnie's face lit with understanding. "And proven it's a love match." Her fingers stilled on her cheeks. "But your secret hasn't been revealed. Not the way the countess intended for it to be."

Of course. Cristina knew him. Damn her but she

did. He was to come here and push Minnie away. In return, she'd tell all of London about the Duke's secret gaming hell. But of course, Cristina had underestimated Minnie. At least this is what he hoped was true. "Why doesn't she just tell London herself? Why would she attempt to have you share?"

"Everyone knows the two of you were once engaged. It's much more believable if it comes from another source."

He stared at Minnie, another piece clicking into place. "And if she thought I was courting you, she'd want to end that relationship. It wouldn't do to see me happy."

Minnie looked back at him, the corners of her eyes crinkling. "Well the joke is on her, then. We were never, nor will we ever court."

His own insides twisted. Which was ridiculous. He'd been the one to openly tell her he wasn't interested. And he'd come here accusing Minnie of plotting against him. He couldn't also be considering marriage. But something inside of him wanted to correct her. "I suppose I have no choice but to attend her party and confront her. This has to come to a stop before anyone else is hurt."

Minnie looked down at her lap. "Good plan. I wish you luck."

"Are you attending?" Somehow, he wanted to see

Minnie and Cristina together. If he saw them, he'd know for certain that Minnie wasn't involved.

She shook her head. "For several reasons, I don't think that's wise."

"Thank the lord," the chaperone said from the corner.

He bent forward, dropping his voice to a whisper. "Not that I blame your chaperone, but she doesn't like me much."

Minnie raised her brows. "You did just accuse me of subterfuge." Then she leaned closer too. "But in this case, it's the countess she doesn't care for."

He rubbed his hands along his thighs. "If you come, we might be able to get more information on Emily and Jack."

"Such as what?" Minnie said at the same moment the chaperone gasped.

"We could ask Cristina what she said to Emily that night." He held his breath. It was a thin argument at best.

Minnie shook her head. "I don't think so, Your Grace. "I know what the countess said. The answers I seek aren't there."

He dropped his voice so the chaperone couldn't hear. "Please Minnie. I need your help."

She threaded her fingers together. "Tag, people

are already taking notice of how much we're seen together."

So that was the issue. "Bring your family and your chaperone. We'll make certain we're not seen together."

She stopped, her face pulling taut as she smoothed her skirts. "All right, Tag. I'll attend. I pray that I do not regret this."

"Thank you," he answered. Had he just won or played right into their hands?

CHAPTER ELEVEN

MINNIE STOOD in her favorite ballgown of silk ivory staring at Tag across the room. Her mother, aunt, and cousins chatting behind her.

"Minnie." Ada tapped her shoulder. "Another lord just passed and you didn't even notice him."

"So?" she asked still looking at Tag, he stared back from across the room.

"So?" Ada huffed. "So. He was looking at you, but you never made eye contact with him so he kept walking instead of asking you to dance."

"Who?" She finally looked at her sister. She didn't want to be distracted by Tag. First, he'd told her he wouldn't marry her, and he'd accused her being in league with that she-devil, the Countess of Abernath. Then he'd had the audacity to ask for her help. Which she'd granted. Why had she done that?

And why was she staring at him instead of taking advantage of this opportunity? She should be using this night for her own gain not for his. She drew a breath as her gaze clashed with his again.

"For heaven's sake, Minnie. Just go talk with him." Ada looped her arm through hers. "You're terribly dull when you're not paying a bit of attention."

"Who?" Minnie looked at her sister, worried Ada was dragging her off to some random man's side.

"Stop asking ridiculous questions. It isn't like you at all. We're going to see Darlington, of course. The man you can't keep your eyes off of."

"We can't see him," she hissed. "People are getting the wrong idea."

Ada sniffed. "If you ask me, they're getting the right idea."

Minnie pulled her arm from her sister's grasp. "What idea is that?"

"What is wrong with you? You've asked more questions in the last five minutes than you did the whole of last year." Ada waved her hand toward Minnie's head. "It's as though someone has taken your mind."

"No one has taken my mind." She reached for her sister's arm and started pulling. "I'm worried about Emily and Jack and…"

"Liar," Ada whispered. "Tonight isn't about them. It's about you and that duke. You're..." Ada drew in a deep breath. "You're in love with him."

"Love?" she asked and then realized she had asked another question. "Don't be ridiculous. I hardly know him and what I do understand about him I don't like."

"Well, cousin Mary says that he convinced you to come tonight against her recommendation." Her sister notched her chin as though that explained everything.

They were making their way across the room, Minnie attempting to move through the crowd. She hadn't seen Tag but she searched the spot where he'd been. He wasn't there any longer. Drat. Disappointment squeezed her chest. "He's here to speak with our hostess and..." She needed a reason why she'd come. "And I thought he might learn more about Emily. That's all."

Ada lightly grasped her shoulder. "Look. I know I'm pushing tonight. You know me, this isn't my strong suit. But you've been spending a great deal of time with Darlington. If he's the man you want, we should make a plan."

Minnie stopped. Was Darlington the man she wanted? Thank goodness she hasn't said that out loud. She caught her lower lip with her teeth. She came at his request. And despite everything, he made her heart beat wildly every time he was near.

She thought back to Charleston. He'd been so easy to spend time with, but in retrospect, there had been no spark. Nothing like the breathless excitement she felt whenever Tag Daring was near. His nickname made her warm inside.

"Where are you going?" Tag was suddenly next to her.

She looked up at him as her pulse began thrumming through her veins. "I was coming to speak with you."

He gave a curt nod. "I haven't been able to speak with our hostess yet, so I've nothing to report."

Ada still held her arm. "I've something to report," Minnie said, standing straighter. Her heart began to hammer in her chest.

"What?" He leaned closer, his brow drawing together. "Did you speak to her?"

She shook her head, her stomach atwitter with butterflies. "No, I haven't. What I need to talk about is you and me."

One of his eyebrows arched. "You and me?"

She gave a stiff nod. The truth was, she had no idea what to say. She wanted to reach out and hold his arm for support. Strange, even when nervous about him, she also drew comfort from Tag's presence. "I—"

"Minnie loves you," Ada blurted, tapping on her arm.

"Ada," Minnie pushed out, turning back to her sister as heat filled her cheeks. How could her sister be such a ninny? "I never said such nonsense."

"Ada," Tag repeated. "Let's get you back to your family."

Minnie suddenly wanted to hide from him as more heat travelled from her face down the exposed column of her throat. "I should also get back to my—"

"We're taking a turn about the room," he said as she slipped her hand into the crook of his arm. Normally, she'd argue when he began being his bossy duke self. But this time, she flushed with satisfaction. Her sister had said the word love and he wasn't running away.

She stole a glance at his profile. Did she love him? Ada said Minnie had been asking a great deal of questions and she was right. But this was the one question that had been muddling her thoughts all night. How did she feel about her duke?

———

TAG MADE his way back to Minnie's family, making a formal request for Minnie's attention. While it was assumed they stay in the public ballroom, he had no intention of remaining in the public eye. A private conversation was required after Ada's outburst. Was it true? Did Minnie love him?

His entire body jolted with energy at the very idea. His teeth clenched. He could not get so wrapped up in emotion that he made a poor decision. He'd made that mistake already with Lady Abernath. He would not allow himself to do so again.

As they reached the corner of the room, he spotted an open door out to the garden. It was away from the large main doors and he moved toward it, Minnie following his lead without complaint.

Which was honestly odd. But as he slipped out the door, he guided her into the shadow beyond the lit room. A hundred questions crowded into his thoughts. Did he love her? Did she love him? Should he do as Jack said and marry Minnie? What if she was just manipulating him as every other woman in his life had done?

But none of those questions made it past his lips. Instead, her hip brushed his and he reached for her waist, pulling her against his body. She pressed to him, molding her soft curves against his hard flesh.

"Tag," she said, her voice catching.

He answered by dropping his head down and capturing her lips with his own. This kiss was not soft, like the last. He kissed her hard, molding their mouths together. Minnie responded by wrapping an arm about his neck, pulling him closer still.

Without thought, he slanted his mouth to push hers open and his tongue brushed hers. Her knees gave out and he tightened his grip on her waist. But as he repeated the motion, her tongue met his sending sparks of pleasure sizzling along his flesh.

She curled her fingers into his hair as the kiss lengthened, their tongues dancing together, their breath mingling. Tag had never kissed a woman with so much...fire. And Minnie returned every heated touch with equal amounts of burning passion.

"Minnie," he begged as he finally lifted his mouth from hers. "Tell me what to do."

"What do you mean?" she asked finding his mouth again.

He kissed her for several more seconds before he pulled back. "Do you feel some affection for me? Could you see yourself with me? Tell me that you do and then we can—"

"Do you have some affection for me?" she asked but he could already hear the change in her voice. Somehow the emotion had cooled.

119

He swallowed. "I don't know yet." She started to pull away but he held her firm. "Listen."

She stilled. "I'm listening."

"What Lady Abernath did to me. What my own parents..." He let out a groan of irritation. He was ruining this. "I can't trust myself. I'm no good at choosing."

She softened, then. Her body fitting to his, her hand cupping his cheek. "I understand. I really do. When Lord Charleston didn't propose, it rocked my confidence to the very core. My mother's threat is the only thing that's started me moving again."

"You understand me." He drew in a ragged breath, dropping his forehead to hers. "I knew you did."

"I do." She lifted herself higher to kiss his lips, a lighter touch as her fingers ran along the front of his jacket. "Which is why I won't tell you what to do. You're one of the strongest men I know. You'll figure it out for yourself."

"What?" He'd wanted her to say the words. *Marry me, Tag. Marry me and I'll erase all those mistakes from your past.* Instead, she'd pushed the decision back on him.

"You heard me," she replied. "Ada is right. Those types of questions are annoying."

He pulled his head back. "Now you're calling me annoying?"

She slid her fingers down his neck. His eyes drifted closed at the touch. Even now, he wanted her to touch him forever. "Let me ask you something. What would you have said if my response had been, '*Yes, Tag. You should marry me.*'" Her palms slid over his chest. "Would you have presented an offer to my family or would you have gone running the other way?"

His head reared back. "You think I was trying to trick you?"

"It's an accusation you made against me just the other day." She fisted the lapels of his coat in her hands.

He let out a deep guttural noise of dissatisfaction. "Well now I'm glad we'll never know what I would have said. It's clear, despite our passion, we can't trust one another."

"I suppose we can't." she answered but he heard her voice quiver. "I shouldn't have come tonight." She slipped from his arms and this time he let her go.

"Maybe you shouldn't have." He straightened, his hands clenching at his side.

She huffed then, pushing at his chest. "You asked me, remember."

He winced, holding her hand against his jacket. "I did. You're a very quick study of people and situations. I'd hoped to engage you in a conversation with Lady Abernath and get your opinion on her motives. Why is she trying to exact revenge now? What involvement did she have with Jack and Emily?"

Her fingers relaxed against him, flattening. "Let's go then, shall we?"

"Go?" He paused, a vision of climbing into his carriage with her and driving away, flitting through his mind.

"To find our hostess. You've asked and so you shall receive."

He grimaced as Minnie reached for his hand and pulled him from the shadow. Lady Abernath was the actual last person he really wanted to talk to. If he were smart, he'd likely stay here with Minnie all night. Until...what? Until they were discovered and forced to marry?

He shook his head. He'd come here to find out why Cristina was still tormenting him after all this time and he'd puzzle it out one way or the other. His feelings about Minnie were tomorrow's problem. Tonight, he needed to face a specter from his past.

CHAPTER TWELVE

MINNIE LOWERED her free hand to cover her stomach as they slipped back into the party and continued their circle about the room.

She should return to her family and leave Tag to face his own problems. But somehow, she was unable to deny him when he asked for help. This wasn't new for Minnie. She did the same for her family, but it wasn't normal for her to feel so compelled to help friends. Though Tag was more than just a casual acquaintance.

Besides, helping him might get her answers about Emily. At least that's what she was repeating to herself.

She thought back to Ada's comment. How deep did her feelings run? She tucked her nose into his shoulder, drawing in his spicy male scent of sandalwood and pine. Her insides danced with excitement and pleasure.

Did she love him? Her eyes drifted closed for a moment as he continued to lead her around the room. Dear God, she did. The idea settled over her like a blanket. Warm and so satisfyingly heavy. Like she was tucked securely in her feelings. Never had she experienced anything like this.

Odd considering her first response to him had been passion, scorching in its heat. The attraction was still there, and somehow it only fueled her feeling of deep affection.

Funny, she'd thought she'd been secure with Lord Charleston. That had been a shadow of the emotion Tag brought out.

"What are you thinking?" he rumbled, the sound coming from deep in his chest and reverberating through her.

She held his arm tighter, her mind searching for an acceptable answer. "I was wondering how we arrived here. I don't mean at this ball. But the first night I met you, we didn't get along at all and now..."

He drew in a sharp breath and held it in his chest. She could feel his expansion and her own body contracted to accommodate him. "Now what, Minnie? What are we now?"

She opened her eyes again, meeting his in a long stare. "You still want me to tell you?"

He let out his breath, the rush of air, somehow changing their shape. "No, I know what's happening between us. I need to decide what to do about it."

Her own brow crinkled. She knew what was happening to her. But she was less certain about him. "When I was with Lord Charleston, I thought I understood perfectly. I was wrong."

He stopped then, leaning closer, his nose near touching hers. "You've your own insecurities to face." They'd reached the hallway back to the grand stair. It was quieter here, most people having now moved into the throng of the party. Tag pulled her off to the side. They were still visible to the crowd but their quiet voices were insulated by the noise around them.

"I do," she replied. "But today, we're addressing your past, aren't we?"

"Oh my," a female voice purred. "Digging up old skeletons, are we?"

Minnie looked to her right and there stood the countess, the picture of cold beauty with her blonde hair and her pale blue eyes. Eyes that creased in the corners in a way they hadn't the last time she and Minnie and met. "I hope not," Minnie answered softly. Tag had gone still next to her.

"What part of his past, specifically?" The other woman moved closer. "Has he shared our history with you?" Lady Abernath scanned them both, Minnie's hand still tucked in his arm. Tag tucked her partially behind his body.

Minnie didn't respond. While he had told her a bit, she knew there must be more to the story.

"I don't want to discuss the past," Tag rumbled. "I want to know why you sent Lady Emily to find Jack that night."

Minnie gasped in a breath but closed her mouth quickly to cover it. She'd thought Tag had been fibbing when he'd said he'd come to find answers about Lady Emily and Jack. That had been an excuse to convince her to attend. But clearly, he'd meant what he'd said.

"How is the happy couple?" She smiled, her lips curling in an almost cruel curve. "Jack was so desperate for love. I'm not surprised he chose a simpering debutante. But not to worry. I'm sure they'll both find other candidates. At least, Lady Emily will."

Minnie's insides itched with irritation and she straightened. The countess clearly did not know everything. She was unaware that Jack and Emily had eloped. Minnie would just as soon keep that information to herself. "Emily is far from simpering."

The countess pierced her with an assessing glare, her eyes travelling up and down Minnie, but Minnie refused to shrink under the scrutiny. "Well, you're no weakling, are you?" The countess moved closer. "Tag did always like a strong woman."

The use of Tag's given name was like a hit to the stomach and she bent a bit. Minnie had grown accustomed to the name and she considered it hers. "Some things never change. Then again, I don't go around attempting to hurt innocent people, so perhaps strength is where our similarities end."

The countess's mouth pressed into a thin line. "They don't end there, I can assure you. Soon you'll be another woman that the Duke of Daring leaves in the dust. Just like he did me." Her face had grown hard, her cheek bones even more prominent as her mouth pressed into a thin line. "Did he tell you the part where he left me alone to fend for myself or the part where he left me with a child in my belly to raise?"

She felt Tag stiffen. "That isn't the story and you know it."

"Isn't it?" The other woman sneered. Then she looked at Minnie again. "Woman to woman, stay away from him. He'll bring you nothing but heartache."

Minnie felt her mouth tremble. She pressed her lips tight together to keep the vibration from showing. "Forgive me, but I do not need advice from you."

"Oh?" The countess steepled her hands. "Well, a warning then. I'm going to tell all of London about Daring's little club. My current plan is to share your visit there."

Minnie felt the blood drain from her face. She wouldn't marry Tag or any man in England if it meant her cousins and sister would likely experience the same fate. No, Minnie couldn't let that woman ruin their future. She had to protect them.

"You wouldn't dare," Tag growled. "It's bad enough that you nearly destroyed me, now you're bringing several innocent parties into this."

"I nearly destroyed you? Have you met my husband? I was forced to marry that odious man because of you." Her lips curled over her teeth.

"Perhaps you should have considered that before you took a lover during our engagement." Tag fired back.

Minnie could feel him tremble. Was it anger or hurt? Inwardly, she shivered as she looked at his face. He was as pale as she felt, though his shoulders were pulled back straight.

"A mistake." The countess waved her hand. "A good man would have married me despite my indiscretion."

Minnie's mouth hung open before she snapped it closed. "You've lost your mental faculties," she said without realizing she'd spoken out loud.

Lady Abernath sneered, her lip curling up on one side. "And you're about to lose your reputation. I knew you'd go racing to that club just as I knew you wouldn't be able to resist my invitation tonight. When I tell the world, that I saw you at his establishment, no one in London will touch you."

Minnie didn't take kindly to threats. Never had. Her back went straight as an arrow. She'd not allow the countess to intimidate either of them. It was time to fight back.

————

TAG WANTED to throw himself in front of Minnie. Unfortunately, though not close enough for anyone to hear them, they were in plain sight of the party. Surely the crowd would notice if he bodily covered Minnie.

Perhaps he didn't care. Part of him wanted to marry her, keep her by his side. With one twist he could silence the voices of doubt that said she'd never love him.

Amazingly, he could barely focus on the Countess of Abernath. She'd angered him in this discussion, in that she threatened Minnie, and he was worried on Minnie's behalf but looking at her, he felt nothing. Not even anger at their past. Of course, he'd like for Lady Abernath to disappear forever, but that was the extent of his feelings.

"I don't care," Minnie said next to him. "Do your worst."

What? He looked at her then. "Minnie," he growled.

The countess let out a cackle. "I know him, dear. He'll not marry you to save you. Don't say that thinking he'll stage a rescue."

Minnie didn't bend. In fact, she appeared to grow taller. "I don't need him to rescue me. Not from you. If you try and out the club, I shall tell everyone that you're lying. That in fact we went to Jack's home. I had a chaperone."

Surprise, gratitude, warmth spread through him. She was going to lie to protect his club. His mind could barely process the details, a sluggish haze making thoughts difficult. "You will not fabricate the truth for me."

Lady Abernath's lip curled. "You can say what

you want. The seed of doubt will be planted. No man of worth will touch you."

Minnie shrugged. "Spinsterhood suits me. Now if you'll excuse me, my family is waiting."

Then she slipped her arm from his and started across the room. Tag turned to follow her, but suddenly Lady Abernath was in front of him. "Feisty, isn't she?" She gripped his arm with a strength Tag wouldn't have thought possible. "That's how you like them, isn't it? Then they're strong enough to withstand all the hurt you rain down on their heads."

Tag stared at the woman he'd once thought he cared for. Cristina was as deep-down angry with him as he'd once been with her. "I don't understand what you get from this. You wronged me."

"Yes, I made a mistake, but you left me with your child." Her fingers dug in even harder.

"My child?" This time it was his lip that curled. "I know you weren't a virgin. Were you already carrying that baby? Or did you and your lover conceive after I proposed?"

She barred her teeth. "How dare you. Do you have any idea what it was like to be alone and pregnant?"

"Do you have any idea what it was like to find the woman I loved cavorting with another man?"

She let go of his arm as suddenly as she grabbed

it. "You don't understand. You never did. After I ruin your precious Minnie, she'll see things my way. You might slip through the noose this time but once she agrees to help me, you'll suffer." She stared at him with hatred oozing from her eyes. "That, I promise you. One way or another, you'll suffer as I did."

He stood straighter. "Cristina, I've already suffered at your hand. More than I could ever say." Pointing his finger, he paused, adding weight to his words. "But you'll not hurt Minnie. I'll see to that."

She let out a loud, cold laugh. "You won't. When it comes to your feelings, you're a complete coward."

Tag clenched his fists. Of all the words Cristina had thrown at him, those hit the mark. He hadn't been a coward with her. He'd given Cristina his whole heart. But with Minnie, he hadn't been brave at all. What did he intend to do about it?

First, he needed to find Minnie and make sure she was all right. He pushed through the crowd, to the spot her family had carved out earlier but they were already gone.

Not wasting a moment, he called for his carriage but he didn't return home. It was a bold move, but he made his way straight for the Chase residence. A man did not arrive at a woman's home late in the evening if he didn't have intentions, but he didn't care.

His carriage rumbled up to the door and he didn't even bother to wait for the footmen. He dashed out of the carriage and up the steps, banging the knocker several times.

The butler opened the door and ushered him inside. "Your Grace." He gestured to the drawing room. "How can I be of service?"

Tag stopped. He hadn't thought this through at all. "I would like to speak with—"

"Your Grace," Mrs. Chase called from the top of the stairs. "Is that you?"

"Yes," he answered relieved. "I was delayed and when I returned to your party, you were gone. I was concerned for Miss Chase. I…" He didn't know what else to say.

Mrs. Chase started down the stairs, smiling indulgently. "Of course you were worried. I told her we shouldn't leave, but she didn't feel well. Sudden headache." Mrs. Chase reached the bottom of the stairs. "I do hope she'll be well enough to sit through her calling hours tomorrow."

Tag nodded. "I'll be certain to come." He desperately needed to speak with Minnie.

CHAPTER THIRTEEN

MINNIE SAT BY HER WINDOW, her hands wrapped
about her stomach, Ada and Diana splayed across
her bed.

"Why did you agree to fall on your sword for
him?" Diana asked, her voice rising with each word.

Minnie shook her head, her hands tightening on
her waist. "We were both going to be ruined. It was
the only thing I could think of that would save one
of us." She turned back to them. "But you're all in
danger. The countess knows all of us were at the
Den of Sins."

Her words were met with silence, but out of the
corner of her eye, she saw Ada and Diana slowly rise
to sitting. "She knows."

Minnie looked over at them. "She must have
followed us. She said she knew that we would go to

the club. She was playing us the entire time." Minnie felt like such a fool. Why had she not realized that the night they'd stormed from the ball and went headlong into a seedy part of London to a club no respectable woman should be at?

"What are we going to do?" Ada whispered.

"Marry. Quickly." Minnie answered. "Or don't and prepare yourself for spinsterhood as I am." She stood then. "I've already amended myself to my fate. And if I can, I'll take the fall for all of us. I'm still thinking. But you won't change my mind about Lord Darlington so don't try."

Diana let out a short laugh that held little humor. "I wouldn't dream of changing your path. I know better than that." Diana stood too and crossed to Minnie. "You make a habit of tossing yourself in harm's way to help those you love but are you sure you want to do this for him?"

"Of course, she does," Ada answered. "She's fallen in love."

"Ada," Minnie huffed. "Would you stop announcing that?"

"Tell me it isn't true." She stood too, placing her hands on her hips. "You're my sister. I know you and I know when you deeply care about someone."

Minnie's shoulders fell. "It's true." Her head dipped down. "But I need you to know he's been nothing but clear that he doesn't want to marry. He hasn't misled me in any way." She looked out the window again into the dark night. She couldn't blame him at all. It was her own foolish heart that had gotten her into this situation and she doubted she'd be able to extract herself from it.

"Do you think he'll change his mind? Knowing that you were willing to sacrifice yourself?" Diana touched her arm.

Minnie shook her head. "I can't explain it, but he's not the marrying kind. Lady Abernath knows it too. She said nearly those words." Minnie spun then, and grabbed Diana pulling her in for a hug. She knew what she had to do and she was prepared to do it, she just needed a little comfort first. "Diana, I need you to help me puzzle out how we're going to keep Grace, Cordelia, and Ada safe. My head isn't as sharp as it normally is and…" She buried her face in her cousin's shoulder.

Diana wrapped her in a tight hug. "Of course, we're going to keep them safe. Nothing's happened yet. What you need is some sleep. Tomorrow, all the answers are going to come to us."

Minnie nodded and Diana let her go, rubbing Minnie's arms as she backed away.

Suddenly, Minnie's door banged open. "You won't believe it." Her mother rushed in, her cheeks a dark shade of pink. "The Duke of Darlington just stopped by to make sure you were all right."

"Mother." Minnie's head gave an actual throb. "You're getting your hopes up. I've told you he's not going to offer."

Her mother sniffed. "You're wrong." Then she paused. "What's your back-up plan if he isn't?"

"Mother," Ada called. "Minnie doesn't feel well. We should discuss this in the morning."

Her mother nodded. "Fine. But His Grace said he would return tomorrow, see that you're ready." Then she turned to go back out the door.

Minnie sighed with relief. Her mother was just too much tonight. "I will."

At the door, her mother looked back over her shoulder. "And Minnie. Come up with another suitor. I meant what I said. You'll be settled before the season begins." Then her mother left, closing the doors behind her.

Minnie looked over at Ada. "She is going to be so disappointed."

Ada nibbled her lip. "Forget about her. It's you I'm worried about."

Minnie was concerned too. She'd just ruined her future, burned it to the ground without even a puff of smoke. What would she do with the rest of her life?

———

TAG JOGGED down the steps of Minnie's home and approached his carriage. "Home, sir?" The driver called.

"No," he answered. "Take me to the club."

The drive was short because the streets were nearly empty. As Tag stared out the window, he thought about Minnie and what she'd done this evening. Scrubbing his head with his hands, he squeezed his eyes shut.

He wasn't as quick with his words as she was, but that didn't stop his gut from filling with guilt. He'd left her to defend him.

Granted, she was the strongest woman he'd ever met, but still. The countess was his battle to fight, not hers. The problem was he hadn't a clue how to do it.

He supposed the only answer was to allow her to tell all of London about his club. Perhaps, it was time to retire from his secret occupation. He thought back to what Jack had said, about how he was ready for a different life.

Tag pushed his fingers into his eyes. Gambling, women…they suddenly sounded hollow, empty of real meaning and feeling.

The carriage pulled to a stop and he once again

jumped out without waiting for the footmen. They'd pulled up into the alley and Tag knocked on the back door meant only for him and his fellow owners. They had a distinctive knock that allowed the guards to quickly discern who was trying to gain entrance.

The guard opened the door, ushering Tag inside. He made his way down the narrow hall where he could already hear the male voices of his friends, likely counting the night's earnings. Stepping into the room, he closed the door firmly behind him. "I need to talk with you."

Four sets of eyes turned back to him.

Malice was the first to speak. "You look like hell."

Tag narrowed his gaze. "What does that have to do with anything?"

"He's not pissed," Exile added. "But he looks like he's been drinking."

"And after that, dragged through the streets," Vice said with a smirk.

"What are you all bloody talking about?" he growled, annoyed they weren't getting to the heart of the matter.

Bad cleared his throat. "Daring, your hair is a mess. Your eyes are red and puffy and your shirt front is all wrinkled."

Tag looked down at himself. Well, they'd arrived at the issue after all. "I've had a rough night."

"I'd never have guessed," Malice said with a curl of his lip.

Tag shot him a wicked glare. "But I haven't been drinking, just so you know, when I swing at your face, I won't miss."

"Of course you haven't been drinking," Vice tipped back in his chair, his blond hair perfectly arranged to wave back from his face. "Your trouble tonight is of the female variety."

Tag clenched his fist at his side. "It's not what you think."

"How do you know what I think?" Vice raised one eyebrow.

"Stop fecking teasing him." Exile banged his hand on the table. "Tell us what happened already."

He did. All of it. Well, he left out the kiss with Minnie. Somehow, he didn't want to share that with them. What happened between himself and her wasn't any of their business. But he told them about the countess's threats and about how Minnie had defended him.

His story was met with absolute silence. Not one man spoke as he finished talking. "Well," he snapped. "What do you think? What should I do?" When had he become so damn indecisive?

Malice spread his hands across the table. "Just so we're clear. Not only is the Chase woman hiding our secret, but she's going to risk her own reputation to protect us?"

His shoulders hunched. "I can't let her do that, you all understand that, right?"

No one answered. Which Tag took as a sign of agreement.

He scrubbed his scalp again. "You'll have to replace me, or not. Buy out my shares." With the words, the hectic feeling inside calmed. "I'm going to marry her. I need to keep her safe. I can't allow her to ruin her entire future for a fecking gaming hell."

Exile nodded. "That's the smartest thing you've said since this entire affair began."

"What does that mean?" Bad growled out, his dark brow pulling low over his eyes.

Exile, a massive Scot, didn't even blink. "It means that the woman is willing to give up her entire future to protect that lug over there. He's a duke. He has to marry. Can you think of a better woman to raise your children?"

Again. Silence.

Tag smoothed out his dark hair. "Exile's right. It's my duty to beget children, I can't deny that she'll make a loyal wife." He also couldn't deny that she was nothing like Lady Abernath. Strength aside, she wasn't selfish and mean. Minnie was...kind, caring, loyal. The question that plagued him was, could he avoid the sins of his parents? For her sake, he had to be brave and try.

"There's another issue we have to discuss." He cleared his throat. "With Jack married to Emily, at least that's what we assume they are doing, and my marriage to Minnie, I doubt the ladies will share our secret. They're not just protecting us but their own kin." He drew in a deep breath. "But in keeping us safe, they put themselves in danger."

"Damn it all to bloody hell," Bad growled out. "I'm not marrying the chit."

Vice put all four legs of his chair back on the floor, the clunk of wood on wood filling the room. "Me either."

"It might not come to that." Daring stepped up to the table. "But you'll protect your assigned lady's reputation and safety or you'll face me."

Malice waved his hand. "Relax, Daring. We'll figure all of this out. Anyone kill a woman before?"

If they touched one hair on a Chase's head..."I'll kill you first."

Malice blinked. "I'm not talking about Cordelia. I already said I wanted to marry her, you egit. I'm talking about Lady Abernath."

That made Tag's head snap back. "We can't go around killing ladies of society, no matter how terrible they are."

Malice nodded. "You're right, of course. I was just testing the theory out loud. Seemed the simplest option."

Vice curled his fingers around his glass. "We can, however, fight fire with fire. The lady has a great many secrets, most of which she would not want her husband to know. And we own a club that services many of the men who likely keep those stories. We could threaten her with her own ruin should she try to hurt us or the Chase women."

Daring relaxed, the knot of tension in his chest unfurling. "That's a bloody good idea. We'll start first thing tomorrow night."

"Bonus, you don't have to marry if you don't want," Bad said, standing and slapping Tag on the back. "No need to retire."

He shook his head. "As Exile said. I don't know where I'd find a more loyal woman. I shall marry her anyway. I am going on thirty after all." He was eight and twenty. Past time for a man of his station to settle down. And he suddenly had the urge for a quieter life.

"Loyalty?" Bad shrugged. "That's one of the least interesting reasons for marrying I've ever heard."

The men all laughed. Even Tag. He was sure there were parts of being married to Minnie that were going to be quite interesting indeed. The only problem. He hadn't actually asked her yet. But surely she'd welcome his advances. He was rescuing her, after all. Surely, she'd appreciate his request for her hand. But his gut niggled with doubt. He'd already hinted that he'd marry her and she had not been all that eager. Would she refuse his offer?

CHAPTER FOURTEEN

MINNIE PATTED HER CHEEKS, then touched the bags that were surely present under her eyes. She'd hardly slept.

Her mother had insisted she attend her calling hours, and as Minnie hadn't yet plucked up the courage to tell her mother she might be ruined, she had no choice but to do as she'd been bid.

Footsteps outside the door made her shift in her seat. Tag was supposed to come visiting this morning. Not that they could discuss anything of any importance with her cousin in attendance.

But somehow, seeing him might make her feel better. Or worse. She didn't know yet. On the one hand, she'd gotten the impression that if she said the word, he'd marry her. That would certainly make her mother happy.

Minnie's own heart jumped. Marrying Tag would make her happy too. At least for a while. But she didn't want him to marry her because he was obligated to do so. Or because she'd coerced him into it. She wanted a man who wanted her.

Even Lord Charleston had granted her that grace. Until he hadn't, of course. Perhaps that was her issue. She didn't want a man who was soft about his feelings for her. Not after the last time. He either wanted her or he didn't. She'd not accept anything less.

The door swung open and her butler gave a slight bow. Minnie held her breath as she waited to see Tag.

"Miss Chase, Lord Charleston is here to see you."

Her breath came out in a rush of air that made her shoulders hunch forward. "I beg your pardon?"

"It's me," a male voice called from behind her butler. "Please say that you'll see me."

She clenched her hands in her lap. What was Lord Charleston doing here? She nibbled the inside of her lip as she held in a sigh. "Of course, my lord."

The butler stepped to the side and her former suitor entered. Minnie's brow drew together. Had his shoulders always been that narrow? His blond hair flopped over his forehead as he tucked his chin into his neck to look down at her. "It's good to see you again."

She pressed her lips into a tight smile. "And you."

"May I sit?" he asked, pulling at his coat.

Minnie gave a small nod. "Of course."

Clearing his throat, he perched on the edge of the chair. He crossed one leg over the other than uncrossed them only to lift the other leg and cross them again. Minnie tried not to sigh. A month ago, two months ago, she would have welcomed Lord Charleston here. She'd fancied herself in love. But now? What she'd felt for him was like. a drop compared with the well of emotion Tag brought out in her.

"I've some terrible news to share with you." He swallowed, his Adam's apple bobbing. "My mother passed this past winter while at our country estate."

Minnie's eyebrows went up. She couldn't help it. "I'm sorry for your loss. I know how important she was to you."

He waved his hand, his gaze dropping to the ground. "I'm lost without her."

Minnie gave a tight nod. She'd imagine he was. "I'm sure you'll recover in time."

He raised a hand. "That's what I've come about actually."

That surprised her. She leaned forward studying his face. "I'm not sure I know what you mean?"

He scooted forward a little further in his chair. Minnie had a moment where she was afraid he might tip out. "Miss Chase." Then he dropped his voice. "Minnie."

She sat back. He'd never been so informal. "Yes?"

"I'd like to request your hand in marriage." He slid from his chair then, dropping down to one knee and taking her hand. "Nothing would make me happier than to make you my wife."

Minnie tried to speak but words failed her. What came out was a series of gurgles and single syllables. Finally, she drew in a deep breath. "Lord Charleston, this is very sudden. I don't know what to say…"

"Say that you'll think about it. Please." He squeezed her hand.

Minnie looked into his pale blue eyes and searched for her answer. She knew what her feelings toward this man were, this was not a love match. But she also knew exactly what she'd be getting. A husband who would bend to her will while shielding her from society's scorn.

She frowned. By contrast, Tag filled her with the sort of heat and light that left her breathless. But he also didn't want to marry her and would have to be coerced into the union. How would she feel about that when his initial interest in her waned? Would he resent her for trapping him? Would she hate him for being at the club when she wanted him home?

She slipped her fingers from Lord Charleston's grip. "I'll think about it."

"Will you now?" Tag rumbled from the doorway.

She looked up to see the butler staring at her with wide eyes, Tag's face visible over the top of Mr. Winston's head.

His eyes were narrow slits as he stared back at her and Charleston.

"I will." She straightened her shoulders, energy sizzling through her.

Tag stormed around the butler, not waiting for the formal invitation to enter the room. "I recall making a similar offer last night and I was not met with the same favorable reaction."

"He proposed?" Lord Charleston croaked, scrambling up from one knee. "I'd heard he'd been showing interest."

"Had you?" Minnie narrowed her gaze. Had Charleston only been prodded into action because of Tag? She didn't care. She turned back to the ornery duke who was glowering down at them. "And you did not propose."

"I didn't?" He tossed his hands in the air. "What would you call it then?"

She stood, taking two steps towards him and tilting her head back so she was looking into his face. "You told me to decide." Then, without thinking, she poked him in the chest. "What sort of proposal was that?"

———

TAG GRUNTED at the sharp jab. Minnie had a point. And not just her finger. "Do you know how many women would love to have any sort of—"

"Stop right there." She poked again. "I'm not any woman." She took a step back, crossing her arms. "Your proposal gets less romantic by the second."

Damn it all to hell, she had him again. "I can't spar with you. You're too quick for me."

Her shoulders relaxed, just a bit, dropping down. Her mouth softened too. Which immediately reminded him of how soft her lips were against his. Her tongue darted out to lick them and he watched the pink tip skim along the supple flesh. "That's the sweetest thing you've said to me."

"It is not," he grumbled.

Charleston cleared his throat. "So you've another offer?"

Minnie's pressed her lips together. "We are attempting to establish that now, my lord."

"You have another offer," Tag said, shooting the other man a glare. How dare Charleston waltz in here and try to take back the woman he'd rejected months ago? "And you've got some nerve showing back up here. Have you no shame?"

"Your Grace." She touched his arm and sparks skittered along his skin. "It's all right."

"It isn't all right." He turned to Charleston. "You broke her heart. You should be ashamed of yourself."

Charleston flushed a bright shade of red. "I did not intend to hurt you. I just couldn't…"

Minnie let out a sigh. "Stop. You don't have to do this. I'm not upset with Charleston anymore. I understand why he did what he did."

"You do?" he asked as he turned back to her. He'd like to understand. How did a man like Charleston let a woman as magnificent as Minnie go? "The man should have kissed the very ground you walk on."

She nodded. "We're all weighted down by our pasts. Our previous problems keep us from seizing our future."

He shook his head. It was as though she'd looked into his soul.

"You've always understood me," Charleston gushed, standing too. "But I'm ready now. Ready to put my past aside and marry the woman I was always meant to."

Tag couldn't speak and his pulse raised as he stared at Charleston. The man was stealing his life right out from under his very nose.

"My lord," Minnie whispered. "That was very heartfelt and I can't tell you how much—"

"No." He grabbed Minnie's arm and pulled her so that he was positioned between her and Charleston.

"Your Grace." Her chaperone stood, huffing out his title. "That is unacceptable."

"I quite agree," Charleston added.

"You're done speaking." Tag held up a hand without looking back at the man who fell silent.

"You can't order him about in my home. You don't have the right." She took a step back from him. "I think it's time for you to go."

"Minnie, please. This can't be the way it ends." Her words were like knives in his heart. But somehow. He couldn't say the words that Charleston had so easily uttered. Had the other man stolen his voice? Or Had Lady Abernath taken it? Or perhaps, it was his mother who'd taken his ability to express genuine emotion.

Minnie reached for his hand, clasping his fingers in her own as her eyes crinkled at the corners. She didn't say a word as she leaned closer. "It doesn't have to be."

He closed his eyes. Then opened them again. He

couldn't argue that he was saving her. Charleston's proposal meant she'd have the protection of matrimony. "I...I need...time...I," his mouth pressed closed.

Her fingers slipped from his. "If you will both excuse me," she said, her voice flat as she smoothed her skirts. "I think *I* need time."

Then she raced from the room, her skirts swishing as she went, brushing the door before it clicked behind her.

Tag watched her go. He had the feeling he'd just allowed his past to steal his future. He needed to act quickly if he stood a chance of reconciling the situation.

CHAPTER FIFTEEN

MINNIE RACED up to her room, tears threatening to fall down her cheeks. She clenched her fists as she moved more quickly down the hall. She'd not allow anyone to see her cry.

What was she upset about anyway? She should be happy. With two offers, she might be able to marry before the countess ruined her. Not that she'd accept either of the men. But she'd tell them each privately and not in front of the other.

Somehow, that thought calmed her. She drew in a deep breath as she opened the door of her room.

"Minnie," her cousin, Mary, called from the other end of the hall.

"Oh Mary," she cried, spinning around. "I just realized I left you with Lord Charleston and Lord Darlington."

Mary waved her hand. "Pay it no mind, dear. That's the most exciting five minutes I've witnessed in some time."

Minnie looked at the ceiling. "Glad to have amused you."

Mary chuckled as she made her way down the hall. "I didn't just come up here to further torture you. I come bearing a message."

"Message?" Minnie pressed her hand to her stomach.

Mary nodded. "I have to confess, I didn't much like your duke at first but..." Mary reached for her hand. "I think that he is trying his hardest to be the man you need."

Was he? Minnie wasn't so certain. Did he want her or did he simply engage in typical male competition when he saw another man interested in her?

"Which is why I've consented to carry this missive to you." Mary leaned over and whispered in her ear, "He wants you to meet him in the garden at nine tonight."

Minnie gasped. "You consented to give me this message?"

"I did," Mary gave her a mischievous smile that made her eyes dance. "If you're caught, I knew nothing about any of this."

Minnie gasped. Her proper spinster cousin had

just set up an illicit meeting in the garden? "Mary, what's happened to you?"

Mary winked. "Well, if you do get caught, the worst that will happen is you'll marry a duke. He's already offered. Once your mother learns that—"

"Don't tell her," Minnie hissed. "There will be no stopping her if you do."

Mary reached for her hand and gave it a squeeze. "I'll do my best, but you'd better decide quickly what you intend to do."

Minnie nodded. Mary had a point there. She needed to let Tag go before her mother made the decision for her. Otherwise, she could find herself trapped in marriage with a man who didn't share her feelings.

———

TAG PACED JUST inside the gate as a clock nearby struck nine. Would Minnie come? His fingers were growing numb. While the days were warming nicely, the nights were quite cool still.

One of his horses whinnied nearby. He'd pulled his carriage into the alley next to the Chase family townhouse. The night was too chilly to speak outside and he needed a private setting for this conversation.

Not that he'd planned what he wanted to say. At least not about his feelings. But he did need to warn her about the countess and what he intended to do about her. If he could protect Minnie from this threat, he felt confident, they could proceed with a real courtship. While he struggled to share his feelings, he was sure over time, Minnie would help him. He might not be able to say the words, but he knew how he felt. No woman had ever made him feel the way she did. Not only that, she was honest and forthright, two characteristics sure to help him open up in time.

He stopped pacing as a rustling noise caught his ear. Cocking his head to one side, he peered into the darkness. A soft shape emerged, easing some of the tension that had coiled within his stomach. As the specter moved closer, he caught the distinct flash of bright red hair. "Minnie."

"It's me," she answered.

"You came."

She stepped in front of him, the pale moonlight illuminating her face in a soft glow. She appeared almost other-worldly with her ivory skin bathed in the crisp light. "I came."

He took her hand and began pulling her toward his carriage. "Come on," he reached back to wrap his other arm about her waist. "It's frigid out here."

"Where exactly are we going?" she asked as she pressed into his side.

"Just to my carriage." He couldn't help himself, he leaned down to drop his nose into her hair. One of her hands touched his stomach and that's when he realized, she wore no gloves. Looking at her delicate fingers grazing his waist coat made him tighten as desire sizzled through his belly, settling in his groin.

"Just out of curiosity, where is your carriage going once we are inside?" Her cheek brushed his shoulder.

"Nowhere," he answered, snapping open the door. "Where would we go?"

"I don't know but Emily has disappeared. It seems a question a girl should ask." She gathered her skirts and stepped inside.

Jack and Emily. He hoped they were happy. When Jack had first left, Tag couldn't imagine why. But now, Tag had a better understanding of how life could get in the way of your heart. "You have my word that I'll not ride off to Scotland with you."

"Oh good," she said from the interior as he climbed inside. "I don't think my family could tolerate a second missing woman."

"They'll return soon. I'm sure of it." He reached for her hand as he settled next to her. "If they don't, I'll go find them for you. That is one problem even I can solve and I'm trying to fix the debacle with the countess."

"What do you mean, even you can solve?" she reached for his cheek then, her bare skin resting against his. He pressed into the touch.

"I have to confess. When I was injured, I enjoyed the way you cared for me. My mother was not very maternal. When I was eight, I broke my arm. Do you know what she said to me? 'Don't die. I can't possibly make another heir with your father.'" He swallowed the bitter taste in his mouth.

"Oh Tag," she murmured. "My mother is often difficult but she loves me. How dreadful for you." Then she leaned over and pressed a kiss to his other cheek. He wrapped his arm tighter about her.

"Try to understand, Minnie, no one ever taught me how to show affection. I'm... I'm working on it."

She kissed his cheek again, slower and with more pressure. "I don't know how I could ask for more."

He gave a small grin relaxing into their embrace. "I meant what I said. I need time to learn and I'm going to be the best pupil I can be. I've got a plan to ensure that the countess doesn't hurt you. I'm late, I know."

"Late?" she asked, pulling away.

He reached for a blanket on his other side, shook it out, then wrapped it about her shoulders. "You shouldn't have had to defend me the other night. I should have taken care of you."

She quirked a brow. "I think you know I'm not a damsel in distress."

"I do know that. I…" He'd been about to say, *I love that about you,* but the words stuck in his throat.

"What are you going to do about the countess?" She settled against him again and without thought, he pulled her into his lap. As her soft backside settled against his legs, his need for her intensified.

"Let's just say, she had a string of lovers and some of them owe rather substantial debts to my club."

She gasped softly, her fingers resting against his neck. "You're using her methods against her."

"I've left her be for seven years. But she went too far when she threatened you."

"Oh Tag," Minnie murmured and then her lips pressed to his.

Heat and a warmth that wasn't precisely desire coursed through his veins as she leaned against his arm so that he supported her weight. "You've helped me, Minnie. More than anyone for a long time." He cupped her cheek before sliding his hand down her neck to skim along the neckline of her dress. "That means so much to me."

Gently pushing the wide neck of her gown lower,

he began kissing the trail his fingertips had just travelled.

"I know you appreciate my help," she said between short breaths, his lips kissing along her collar bone. "And thank you for telling me about your mother. My family, we love one another. I never considered how difficult that is for some people."

Of course she understood. It was yet another reason she was perfect for him. Reaching under the blanket, he undid the first several buttons at the back of her gown. The fabric slumped forward and he pushed it further down her arms, revealing her chemise and corset. He began plucking at the strings in the back as he lowered his head and kissed her clothed breast. She gasped and he gently nudged the fabric down to place a light kiss on the tip of her rosy nipple. Her breasts weren't large but they were round and high and perfect to fill a man's hand. He did exactly that and she arched into the touch.

"Tag," She curled her fingers into his scalp as he kissed the sensitive flesh again, then sucked her into his mouth. He did the same to the other as she pressed closer to him, her head tilted back, allowing him access to creamy skin.

Without thought, he began to slide her dress up her legs, skimming his fingers along her calf, over her knee and then up her thigh. She shivered underneath the light touch, her hands clutching at his shoulders.

He reached the apex of her legs and pressed against her mound, the fabric still separating his touch from her. She bucked against him, crying out.

"Shh," he murmured close to her ear. "We don't want anyone to hear us, my love." But he had no intention of stopping. Minnie was spread across his lap, her long legs flowing across the bench seat as she leaned back against him. Having her trust him like this filled his heart with a pleasure he couldn't name. She was beautiful and strong and willing to put herself in his hands.

Tag intended to reward her for such trust. He parted her pantaloons, and grazed her tender flesh with the tips of his fingers. She whimpered, gripping his arms tighter as her legs fell further apart.

Smiling at her response, he found her lips again and gave her a long slow kiss as he repeated the movement with his hand, adding just a bit more pressure. She kissed him eagerly, her hips pushing into his hand.

"Do you like that, love?" he said against her lips.

"Yes," she gasped, "Oh, yes."

He stroked again, creating a rhythm with his hand. He wished he could see her, but that would have to wait for the next time. He'd explore every inch of her body. Then he realized, he was planning a next time and a time after that.

He wanted all of those times and more. Wanted to hear her murmured words of understanding as he shared the layers of his past. Wanted to watch her belly grow with his child and hold her close.

With a startling realization, Tag realized that he loved this woman. Yes, she was strong, strong enough to hold him up when he failed. She was also kind and giving. Hadn't she been willing to sacrifice herself for his benefit? Who had ever done that for him before?

Minnie moaned again as he moved faster, her body shaking with the finish that was building. God, he loved seeing her like this. Truth be told, he just loved looking at her. In the morning light, at night, in the garden, or the drawing room. "Minnie," his voice broke as he held her close. He loved her. And he'd do anything to make her happy. Now how did he convince her of that?

CHAPTER SIXTEEN

MINNIE WAS ABOUT to burst into a tiny thousand little pieces. Break apart. She hoped she'd come back together, but the working part of her brain wondered if she'd ever be the same.

Tag's scent swirled around her so strong and masculine, the sandalwood and pine both erotic and comforting.

He pressed his lips to hers again. "That's it, love. Let go."

"Tag." She breathed him in, the heat of him filling her with warmth. "I..." What did she say? She wanted to tell him that she loved him. That she'd do anything for him if only he'd love her in return.

"I know, sweetheart."

Did he? She couldn't think anymore as she shattered and cried out his name. He held her against his chest, cradled in his arms, his forehead pressed to hers. "That was…"

"Beautiful," he whispered in the dark interior. "A gift I shall treasure always."

She stilled wondering what he meant by that. "As shall I."

He kissed her long and slow, keeping her close. "There is something I have to tell you."

"What?" her body was soft and her muscles sluggish but her mind came back into focus. "What's wrong?"

He gave his head a little shake. "I'm sorry that I didn't do more to protect you the other night at the ball but I'm going to do it now."

She huffed a breath. "I need you to understand. Protection isn't a good enough reason to marry. You'll resent me—"

"No sweetheart, I won't. But that's not what I'm talking about." He kissed her cheeks, her chin, the tip of her nose. This sort of touching was so intimate, that she relaxed back into him. "I've come up with a plan to ensure the countess doesn't say a word about you. It's not that I don't want to marry you, but I want you to have all the choices you can have. You deserve that."

She swallowed, attempting to sit up. So much had been said in that one sentence, she wasn't certain where to begin. "You want to marry me and you want me to have choices?"

He smiled against her cheek. "Let's first focus on my plan with the countess. She's managed to accumulate quite the list of ex-lovers."

"Has she?" Minnie nibbled at her lip. "After tonight, I suppose I see why."

Tag let out a little growl of dissatisfaction. "Minnie, I am the only man who will ever touch you like this."

That made her smile. "We've yet to work out those details."

"We're going to." He kissed her then. "Once I've eliminated the threat to your reputation."

She caught her breath. "I like it when you talk like that."

He still cupped her mound and moved his fingers again as sensation sizzled through her.

"Do you?" he said between kisses on her neck. Then he stopped. "Just be careful. The countess is likely to be upset. Avoid her if you can and let me know what social events you plan to attend. I want to make sure you're safe."

Her body hummed at his touch. "I will." Then she bit her lip. "I'm going to a garden party tomorrow. I've invited Lord Charleston."

He stopped, his hand stilling. "What?"

It was her turn to place a soft kiss on his neck as she wiggled under his fingers. "I need to tell him that I can't accept his offer."

"Oh," he began touching her again. "In that case, carry on. And I'll meet you there."

"Tag," she warned. Part of her wanted him there. He was softer today, more giving and she wanted to know more about this man. But she owed Lord Charleston a private explanation.

"I'll be fashionably late, love." He slid her off his lap and onto the bench as he shifted to crouch down on the floor of the carriage. "Now lay back. I want to know how you taste."

"Oh," she hummed. This was going to be fun indeed.

But the next day, she wasn't as certain.

Minnie thread her arm through Diana's as they circled their picnic spot at Hyde Park. She'd set up a more private meeting with Lord Charleston and Diana was coming as her chaperone. She couldn't damage her reputation now.

"I've never seen a more morose woman who had two marriage proposals." Diana teased.

Minnie had waved her hand. "You make it sound far better than it is. One isn't a real proposal. Charleston means well but…" She sighed. Best not to finish that out loud. He could be just around the corner. "And Darlington has never actually said that he cares for me. I don't want a marriage that is so… one-sided."

"Your mother would disagree. She's completely atwitter that a viscount and a duke have offered for your hand, on the same day."

"Technically speaking, His Grace offered two days ago." Heat filled her cheeks thinking about their time in the carriage last night. "And neither of his proposals were very good."

Diana grinned. "Only you can refuse a duke because he didn't propose the right way. Every other woman would be falling over herself to say yes."

Minnie frowned. "Perhaps that is true. But only because she hadn't thought through all the repercussions of marrying a man who didn't really care about her."

She desperately wished to say yes to Tag. Her heart thrummed in her chest as she thought about his broad shoulders and strong jaw. But she didn't want half of him. She refused to become his wife out of charity. He either wanted all of her or none.

She tossed a lock of hair that had fallen forward back over her shoulder. "You've got me here, Diana. What would you do if you were me?"

Diana winked at her, steering her down a nearby path. "I am you, in many respects. You and I do not make the safe choices, Minnie. We reach for more."

Well that certainly wasn't Charleston. Not that she hadn't decided that on her own already. "You can't think the duke is more?"

"Doesn't matter what I think. I've seen the way you look at Lord Darlington. Never have you looked at another man that way." Diana gave her arm a squeeze.

She let out a sigh. "That's not the question. I know how I feel. What I don't understand is how strongly he does." She twisted her fingers. "I know that Tag would marry me. That he feels an attraction and has the desire to care for me but beyond that…"

"Have you asked him?"

Minnie pressed her lips together. As a matter of fact, she hadn't. Perhaps it was time she did.

———

TAG SAW the party as he approached the garden. He recognized Mrs. Chase and Ada but Minnie was nowhere to be seen. Then he caught sight of a flash of bright red hair as she and Diana slipped down a path.

Excitement coursed through him even seeing her across the garden. Bloody hell, he really was in love.

He changed his course, following behind Minnie. He'd promised her space and he intended to give it to her but he also planned to be there if she needed him. With that in mind, he slipped down the garden path, keeping to the shadows.

"Lord Charleston," Minnie said. "A pleasure to see you."

In that moment, Tag realized he was eavesdropping on her conversation. That had not been his intent but footsteps on the path behind him had him darting behind a bench. For a moment he wondered why on earth he'd just hid. He could walk on a path without worry but then he caught sight of pale blonde hair. Peeking over the top of the wood slats, the profile of the Countess of Abernath came into view.

"It's a pleasure to see you again, Miss Chase." Charleston all but gushed. "I've missed you so and I've been anxiously awaiting the answer to your question."

"Very kind, Lord Charleston," Minnie answered as Tag stood again. The countess had passed and he crept silently behind her. "I wanted to answer you post haste. I—"

"Oh, isn't this just so sweet," Lady Abernath purred, coming up behind the trio. Diana straightened, stepping in front of Minnie. Gads, he'd never known a better group of women.

"What do you want?" Minnie placed her hand on Diana's shoulder, stepping next to her cousin. His Minnie was no wilting rose.

"Did he offer for you hand, Miss Chase?" Lady Abernath purred.

Minnie straightened. "That is none of your concern."

"Oh but it is, Lord Charleston." Lady Abernath waved her pale hand at the other man who took an involuntary step back. "Did you know that Miss Chase was in an illicit club after hours with a group of eligible gentlemen?"

Charleston took another step back. "I beg your pardon?" His eyes darted to Minnie. "This is a lie, isn't it? Your reputation would be—"

"It isn't a lie." Minnie's back was straight as a board.

"Oh," Charleston said, his voice barely audible. Irritation flitted along his skin. Bloody hell, he hoped he hadn't been that weak the last time Lady Abernath had tried to corner him.

"I relieve you of your offer. You're free to go," Minnie added, never looking away from the countess.

Lord Charleston took another step back. "If

you're sure, Miss Chase. I don't mean to offend. I just..." Then he turned and fled.

Lady Abernath shifted, one of her hands cocking on her hip. "I have to confess that I like you. You're strong. In some ways you remind me of myself."

Minnie's lip curled. "No wonder His Grace doesn't want to marry me."

Lady Abernath trilled a laugh, the sound making his blood cold. He stepped forward out of the shadows. "That isn't true at all, I've practically begged you to marry me."

Diana let out a small gasp but Minnie's gaze shifted to him, softening. "Is that what a duke considers begging?"

He stepped past Lady Abernath. "A pleasure to see you again, Cristina." Here in this private conversation, he needed to let her know, he hadn't forgotten the past. "I say that purely for social grace."

She glared at him. "The Marquess of Malicorn told me about your little scheme. It won't work, those men will never tell my husband—"

"It will work." He stepped over to Minnie's side. "Men in debt will do all sorts of things to keep their families safe."

Lady Abernath's lips thinned. "You're blackmailing me."

He gave her a cold smile as he slipped his arm

about Minnie. "Just returning the favor. You're not to speak to Miss Chase ever again."

Lady Abernath's eyes narrowed into slits. "You're trying to tell me what to do. After what you did to me?"

Minnie drifted against his side, her hand coming to his shoulder. "Don't answer."

"You're making a mistake, Miss Chase, curling up against him like a purring cat. He'll never actually marry you. He'll say he will but then—"

Anger made his fingers numb. He gripped Minnie's waist tighter, keeping his grip on sanity. "How dare you. I'd marry Minnie tomorrow if she'd have me. You want to blame me rather than admit your own wrongdoing."

"I didn't deserve what you did." She clenched her skirts. "And if you think marrying her will protect her, you're wrong. I'll see you pay."

Tag drew up to his full height. "You can't hurt us, not without hurting yourself and your husband."

Lady Abernath's lip curled. "You think I care about him? My husband can rot in hell. Your club is going to be ash, your relationship dust, and your friends gone. Mark my words. You think you've won but you've only stirred my ire." She spun about. "I'll see you suffer."

They all watched as she stalked away.

"That was your first fiancée?" Diana asked. "No wonder you were scared off marriage."

Tag couldn't help himself, he barked out a laugh. "That is the absolute truth."

"How worried should we be?" Minnie still looked to the spot the countess had disappeared. "She threatened to ruin me. What do you think she's capable of doing?"

"It doesn't matter. As a duchess you'll be completely safe." He held her tighter to his side, relief flowing through him as she curled into his side.

"We didn't agree to a wedding. You said you were going to eliminate the countess's threat so that we could discuss this."

He stiffened, looking down into her eyes. Why didn't she accept his offer? It hurt that she refused to accept. "I've asked you to marry me multiple times. What more do you want?"

"Tag." She swallowed, her hand coming to his neck. "I love you."

Those words made him freeze. Had anyone in his entire life ever uttered them to him before? Something deep inside him shifted.

Her fingers slid to his cheek. "But I need to know how you feel in return. I…" Her face tightened. "I can't be married to you if you don't feel the same."

She hadn't been holding out on him because she didn't care. She'd held herself away because he couldn't share his heart. "I know I've struggled to express my feelings. No one taught me how. I'm trying."

Her thumb brushed down his cheek. "I appreciate that. We can court. I can teach you…"

No. That simply wasn't good enough. "Come on. Let's go."

CHAPTER SEVENTEEN

"WHERE?" she gasped as Tag pulled her back down the path.

Diana lifted her skirts to keep up. "Whatever is happening, I'm not going to miss this."

Tag didn't look back. "I need to prove something to you right now."

"Now? What?" she asked. Not that he answered where either. She lifted her own skirts as he pulled her along. Part of her wanted to drag her feet and make him explain but another part wanted to see where this was going. "Tag."

He turned back to her then. "You want to know how I feel?"

She nodded, not able to answer in words. There was a light in his eyes she'd never seen before. She'd like to reach out and touch it. "I'm not only going to tell you, I'm going to show you."

"Oh my…" She didn't have a chance to finish.

Diana yelled behind them, "Do wait for me. I can't miss this." Then she lifted her skirts higher. "Grace and Cordelia are going to be so upset they didn't come. I told them they should."

"Diana, please," Minnie called over her shoulder, her heart hammering in her chest.

Tag pulled them back into the midst of the party. Several people sat on blankets, enjoying one of the first truly warm days of spring. "May I have everyone's attention."

"Oh no," Minnie gasped. Tag was not a man to make public announcements. What was he doing?

"Oh yes." Diana clapped behind her. "This is going to be fun."

"I'll remember this," Minnie hissed back.

"Not very long ago, I met Miss Minerva Chase. Since then she's changed not only my life, but my outlook on my past, present, and future."

"Oh, this is wonderful," Minnie's mother called from the crowd. Minnie couldn't even search to find her mother. She was looking at Tag, her eyes already misting over. Was he about to publicly declare his feelings?

"I've resisted marriage. But this woman has changed all that. She has made me want to be a better man. A man who can love with his whole heart. Miss Chase," He turned to her then. His eyes soft around the edges as his hands gripped hers. "Will you do me the honor of becoming my wife? I love you more than words can ever express and I'll do my utmost to prove that to you each and every day."

Minnie opened her mouth to speak, but no words came out. Not only had he declared his feelings but he'd done so publicly. Her eyes itched with unshed emotion. She knew how difficult it was for him to express emotion after what he'd been through. She moved closer, wanting to be near him. Not only had he declared his love, he'd done it in front of fifty people. "I..." She tried but her tongue stuck to the top of her mouth. "I..." She gripped his hands tighter. For the first time in a very long time, she was tongue-tied and shy

Diane nudged her from the back. "Spit it out."

"Yes," She managed to push out. "I'd be honored to be your wife."

"Thank the lord," her mother yelled from the crowd. Then louder. "My daughter's going to be a duchess."

Laughter and cheering rose about them, but Minnie only looked at Tag.

"I love you, Minnie," he said softly. "I have for a while. I'm just not very good at saying these things. You know my past."

This time a tear slid down her cheek. "You did a marvelous job for a man who struggled." Then she leaned in closer. "Meet me at the garden gate tonight and bring a blanket."

He smiled, leaning in close. "If you insist."

Her mother rushed up, wrapping her arms about Minnie and breaking the moment. But Minnie watched Tag watch her. She could see the love shining in his eyes. Tonight she'd show him exactly how much his proposal meant to her.

———

TAG STOOD by the garden gate for the second night in a row. He hadn't brought one blanket, he'd brought seven or eight along with a few pillows. It was just cool enough that all the windows were closed, affording them some much-needed privacy, but warm enough that they could be outside.

He'd hardly thought of anything but her since this afternoon. Everything had come together in his mind. What she needed, why he'd been holding back, and how it was time to let his past go.

Minnie had already showed him the path to a life

filled with love. She'd protected him, comforted him when he'd been hurt, stood up for him against Lady Abernath. Now it was time for him to show her that he was capable of learning and willing to set his past hurts aside.

He'd hoped that he'd reciprocated her strength in love today and he knew, he hoped, what it meant to be a good husband.

She appeared on the path, the moonlight making her easier to see than she had been last night. A crisp white night rail billowed around her and his breath caught. Not only did she look beautiful, her hair in a simple braid, but she'd dispensed of all her layers of clothing. The implication of that choice tightened all his muscles.

She didn't say a word as she reached for him, her hand sliding into his, and he pulled her close, wrapping an arm about her waist. "Are you cold?" he murmured just before he captured her lips with his own.

"No," she said between kisses. "I'm lovely. Just perfect."

Wrapping his other hand below her buttocks, he lifted her into his arms continuing to kiss her in long leisurely strokes of his lips against hers. Minnie wrapped her arms about his neck, sliding her hands into his hair. "What you said today. Did you mean it? You really love me?"

Tag leaned back, assessing her. "It's not like you to be insecure."

"I'm not." She smiled as she brushed her nose against his. "I just want to hear you say it again."

He laughed and, reaching the blankets, lay her down. "I love you, Minnie. I plan to spend the rest of my life showing you just how much."

She sighed, settling back onto his makeshift bed. "See. That wasn't so hard."

He settled his weight on top of hers. "Would you like me to show you all the ways I care?"

"Oh yes," she breathed, her legs spreading to allow his to settle between them.

He kissed her again. This time the touch wasn't slow or light, it was filled with all the passion building inside him.

Minnie responded, her heartbeat quickening against his.

He ran his hands over her body, feeling every dip and curve until they were both panting with desire. As he ran his hand down her legs, he hooked the hem of her night rail and began pulling it up until the fabric pooled about her waist. "I want to see you. All of you," he said against her lips. She gave him a light push and for a brief moment, he worried she was pushing him away but the moment he rose, she grabbed the fabric and sent it sailing over her head. Then she lay back down, arms raised so that he had a full view of her naked body.

"Like this?" she asked, giving him an impish smile.

He swallowed, his eyes running down her slender frame his hand following close behind. "Like that."

Her skin was velvety soft and so creamy in the moonlight, his mouth was dry and his throat clogged. She was perfection, with her perfect mounds for breasts, flat stomach, and small tapered waist. He slid his hand over her hip and then caught sight of the flaming hair that tapered off between her legs. He made a noise deep in his throat as his fingers brushed the curls and settled in her soft womanly flesh between her thighs.

She bucked against him and he pulled his fingers away, yanking off his own waist coat, cravat, and shirt.

He settled against her again, their skin coming together in the most satisfying way. His manhood throbbed. He wanted nothing more than to bury himself inside her soft, waiting flesh, but he held back and began kissing a trail down her body instead. Her pleasure would come first.

———

As his mouth settled over her slit, Minnie gasped, clutching the blankets closer. She wasn't cold. She'd never been hotter in her life but she needed to hold onto something as pleasure rocked through her, tensing all her muscles.

He set a steady pace with his mouth as he slowly inserted a finger in her channel. Her eyesight blurred as little noises of delight fell from her lips. She'd never imagined rapture like this and she started to beg for more. "Please. Tag. I want...don't stop."

She felt his smile as he increased the pace. "Never," he said then drove his finger deeper inside her until she convulsed and then shattered.

As she slowly floated back down, she looked up at him with heavy eyes as he peeled the rest of his clothing off. Raising her arms toward him, she gave him a slow smile. "Come here."

He didn't hesitate. Lowering himself on top of her, his weight settled over her. She gasped in a breath. He was so hard and muscular and yet somehow, he felt like home. "Tag," she whispered. "I love you so very much."

"I love you too." He kissed her as the tip of his manhood pressed to her opening. "Minnie, you've brought love to my life and I don't know how to thank you for it but I'm going to try."

She pulled back, shaking her head. "Just give me yourself. That's enough."

Slowly, he slid inside her. She tensed at the pain but held still. Minnie was not the sort to shy away from a bit of pain. However much it hurt, he was worth it. But she couldn't help but cry out a bit as her maidenhead broke.

He stilled, smoothing back her hair and peppering kisses about her face. "I'm sorry, love. Thank you for such a beautiful gift."

She leaned up and kissed him back. "You're welcome. Is now the appropriate time to ask when our wedding will be?" Then she giggled. She'd meant it as a joke but he grimaced.

"I should have waited but I've already retrieved the special license. I think your family will object to a wedding tomorrow but I'm hoping for the next day."

She stilled, looking up at him. "Tomorrow or the next day?" She held his face in her hands. "We'll begin our life together in a day or two?"

"We've already begun," he said as he slowly moved inside her. "You're mine, Minnie."

They didn't say more as Tag slowly slid out of her

body and then back in. Soon the pain diminished and only pleasure remained.

She didn't need to say that yes, she was his. She showed him with every touch and kiss until her own body begged for release again. When she fell over the edge, he cried out her name, spasming above her.

She held him against her. She'd love this man forever.

EPILOGUE

Two days later...

Minnie stood in the garden only feet from where their blanket bed had been two nights prior. She kept grinning at the spot where Tag had held her in his arms until the wee hours of the night.

"Minnie," he whispered leaning over. "We're about to say our vows."

She blushed, her cheeks surely as red as her hair. "I suppose I feel as though I already said them."

He squeezed her hands. "That's true." Then he looked out over the small gathering of family and friends. "But they don't know that, so do me a favor and look at me. Otherwise they might think I'm forcing you to the altar."

A giggle nearly burst from her throat but she swallowed down. "Forced into marriage by a duke."

He returned her smile. "Could happen."

The magistrate cleared his throat. "If the couple is ready."

Minnie gave a tiny nod. As Tag agreed to love, honor, and cherish her until death do them part, a sense of peace washed over her. She'd managed to marry as her mother requested, or rather insisted, to a man who made her bubble with joy.

"I do," she added as they finished their vows.

"Then I now pronounce you husband and wife."

Tag leaned over, capturing her lips with his. A cheer went up from the crowd, filling the early morning air.

Tag led her back down the garden path and into the house where a wedding breakfast awaited them.

Her hand in the crook of her husband's arm, she closed her eyes. How had the surly duke she'd first met become the man that filled her heart?

When she opened her eyes again, however, she realized several of the guests hadn't followed her into the room. Diana stood in the doorway, holding a note, her lips pursed.

"Diana?" she called.

Her cousin dropped her hand to the side and strode in through the doors. "It's from Emily."

Minnie swallowed a gasp. "What did she say? Is she all right?"

"She's fine." Diana huffed. "All that worry and they are taking a holiday in Scotland after their elopement."

"Did she say why they eloped in the first place?" Tag asked as the Marquess of Malicorn came to stand beside him.

Minnie gave Tag's friend a tight nod of greeting. Tag hadn't invited his other friends to the wedding. He'd said the notice was too short but Minnie suspected this had something to do with the club.

Ada, Cordelia, and Grace joined the group too. Diana snorted before she answered, "She only says that she hopes we understand but they needed to follow the path of true love."

"I think it sounds romantic," Cordelia sighed as she pushed up her glasses.

Malicorn made a choking noise in his throat. "Don't tell me you're one of those ninny-headed women whose dreams are full of romance and true love?"

Cordelia straightened, attempting to look down her nose at him. "So what if I am? It's not your concern."

He said something under his breath that Minnie

couldn't quite catch. She gave her head a shake. It didn't matter. "Did Emily say anything else?"

"Just that they'll be home in a fortnight." Diana refolded the paper, her movements jerky and short. "Does she realize she's left us in a pickle? I mean the countess didn't appear happy with the threat you made."

Tag held up a hand. "We've got her cornered."

"Says you." Diana gave him a look up and down. "She's a predator, you know. They often come out of corners fighting. And that one's got a full set of claws."

Malicorn grimaced. "We'll be ready for her if she does."

"She can't ruin us all, can she?" Grace asked.

Ada squeaked. "I don't think I'm meant to be a spinster."

Tag wrapped his arm about Minnie. "One way or another, we'll keep you ladies safe."

Minnie inwardly winced. She was completely protected as Tag's wife but her cousins and sisters… that was another story entirely.

MARQUESS OF MALICE

LORDS OF SCANDAL

Malice, as his friends fondly referred to him sat on a bench in the garden of the Chase family home, staring at the newly emerging spring flowers that were sprouting from the ground.

His name was Lord Chadwick Hennessey, Marquess of Malicorn, but no one had called him by his given name since his mother had given him it with her dying breath.

Which was likely why he hated being called Chadwick. It held too many ugly memories. He ran his hand through his hair staring at a small green bud struggling to rise up through the dirt. He grimaced. He'd been that flower as a child. Struggling and straining to flourish, the very ground that was supposed to nurture him, pushing him back into the dirt.

He straightened his back, drawing in a deep breath. He wasn't that child any longer. He was a grown man now who never wallowed in self-pity.

Standing, he stared down at the tiny plant. He wouldn't expend emotion on a flower but he could help it. Just a bit. He leaned over and brushed the dirt away from the small plant giving it more room to grow. Satisfaction, spread through his limbs and he let out a long breath as more of the bright green stock came into view.

"Oh," a feminine voice trilled from his left. "My apologies, my lord."

He stopped, his fingers still in the dirt. He'd been caught caring about a tiny plant. Even worse, it was *her* who had made the discovery. His insides tightened. Despite the fact this was only the second time they'd met, he knew the sound of Lady Cordelia Chase's voice without even looking at her.

Malice had carefully fostered a reputation of reckless abandon sprinkled with a healthy dose of sarcastic indifference. He rarely showed emotion toward anyone or anything. He most definitely didn't want Lady Cordelia to think he was a sappy sort. It would give her the wrong impression. "What are you apologizing for?" Malice straightened, giving her a long look as he glared down at her. How odd.

She pushed up her glasses, nibbling at her lip.

"For interrupting. Had I known anyone was out here, I would have come with a chaperone."

He relaxed, his shoulders slumping down. She didn't seem to have noticed that he was aiding tiny plants. "No need to apologize." He cared not if she were chaperoned despite the fact that she was a tender debutante. "How goes the wedding breakfast?"

Cordelia turned back to look at the house. "Very well. If you'll excuse me, I'll just return inside."

"No need." He waved his hand. "I'll escort you back to the wedding breakfast in just a moment."

She cocked her head to one side. "I beg your pardon?"

He ignored her question, instead studying her from top to bottom. Her fair hair was tied rather tightly back from her face. The hair itself looked soft and he wondered how she might look with a looser coif. Her glasses perpetually slid down her nose, likely because it was the tiniest nose he'd ever seen with just a slight upturn at the bottom. When she looked at him over the top of the glasses, her eyes were a striking color of crystal blue like a lake on a sunny day. Quite pleasant.

On their very first meeting, she'd not been wearing the spectacles and had promptly tripped into his arms. She had a nice figure. Curvy without being overly large, and without the dark rims of her glasses, he'd noted the lovely shape of her eyes, large and clear with a gentle upturn at the outside corners. Glasses or no, a man couldn't miss how nice the curve of her mouth was—so full and tempting.

He'd also realized she was a quiet and affable lady who would make an excellent wife.

Unlike many men, he'd made several decisions on that front. First, he planned never to fall in love. Emotions like that were an affliction. As the holder of the title, he was obligated to continue his line, by marrying and conceiving an heir. Not a part of his life he looked forward to.

His parent's marriage had been brief to say the least. Barely a year. He didn't remember his mother, of course, but he couldn't imagine that the union had been a happy one, if his own relationship with his father was any indication. Although his father would swear that all the love he felt had died with his mother. "Tell me, Lady Cordelia. How do you spend your time?" He assumed reading, knitting, and socializing were at the top of her list. All excellent past times for a wife.

She shrugged, inching back a bit. "I don't know. What all ladies do. A little of this and a bit of that."

He stepped forward. Her comment highlighted what he liked about her. She appeared to be a malleable woman. Easy in her temperament which was exactly the sort of woman he needed.

And that was the main reason he was here. Cordelia, along with her sisters, had arrived at their secret club in the middle of the night. Now one of his partners, the Earl of Effington, was married to Cordelia's sister, Emily. But the ladies weren't supposed to be there. In fact, they weren't supposed to know about the club at all.

When Emily had arrived with her two sisters, Cordelia and Grace and her cousins, Minnie and Diana, all hell had broken lose. The men were concerned about the club's secret, the ladies about their reputations. Emily and Jack had almost called off the wedding. And the other men had begun to fear for their club's reputation and continued business. They'd made a thriving financially successful gaming hell by creating an air of mystery about their identities. To make certain this continued, Malice and his friends had decided to watch the ladies and make certain they didn't share their secret.

"Sounds delightful," he said, his thoughts still on their first meeting a few weeks prior.

When Cordelia had nearly fallen directly into his arms, she'd blushed and apologized. He'd held her close, taken off her domino, and studied her face. She was pretty, petite, almost pixie-like. Quiet and unassuming. He'd decided right then. He'd marry her, make an heir and settle her into his country estate leaving her to raise the child. Easy.

She squinted her eyes. "Really? I was thinking a little of this and a bit of that didn't sound like anything at all."

He looked back at her, his mind refocusing to the present. Was the sun reflecting off her glasses or was there a glint in her eye? "Precisely."

Her small pink tongue darted from her mouth and licked her full upper lip, starting in one corner and sliding across the entire bow of her mouth until it finally finished on the opposite side. His insides tightened in the strangest way. He knew what lust was, he was a seasoned man of eight and twenty. He'd had more than his fair share of partners. But Cordelia should have nothing to do with such emotions. Why was his body responding to her? She was the safe and predictable choice.

He'd chosen her so that he'd have a wife he could remain detached from.

"What do you mean, precisely? Precisely what? That doesn't make sense. You don't want me to say anything of consequence?" She narrowed her gaze. "Why do you care what I say at all?"

He frowned. They were already getting off topic. "You're missing the point."

"I don't think I am." She curtseyed. "Now, if you'll excuse me." Lady Cordelia gave a small sniff and then she turned to go.

Malice dropped his hands, his brow scrunching. What the bloody hell was she doing? Letting out a frustrated breath he crossed the garden and grabbed her arm.

———

Cordelia started down the path determined to leave the Marquess of Malicorn where he belonged. In her past.

It wasn't that she didn't like him, precisely. That word made her pause. *Suitable.* He'd used it in the most curious way. He was darkly handsome with a square jaw and features that were disconcerting in their sharpness. Prominent cheekbones and a heavy brow that lent him an air of danger.

She shivered, despite herself. His large frame hinted at muscles that surely were a hazard to any upstanding lady. Both because she knew him to be a man that didn't follow rules and because all his features put together, made him rather...exciting.

As if he were reading her thoughts, he reached out and wrapped his fingers about her arm at the same time he spoke her name. "Lady Cordelia."

She jolted, her insides going silly as she whirled about. "You frightened me."

He immediately dropped his hand. "My apologies. I simply would like to continue our conversation."

Cordelia caught her lip between her teeth. "Very kind of you but I must decline."

He stared down at her, his brows drawing together. She'd thought his eye color was near black but out here in the light, she could see they were far more chocolate in their shade of brown and rather endearing. "Why?"

Her mouth opened as she tried to form words. Why? Was it not obvious? "You are an eligible man and I am an eligible woman. We should not be found alone together. We've enough scandal floating about us already. You know the Countess of Abernath has threatened to expose me and my family for our visit to your club. We should take every precaution to be proper."

He relaxed at those words, his shoulders easing down. "I agree and I appreciate your sense of propriety. It's a most advantageous quality."

Cordelia stilled, his words tumbling about her mind. There it was again. He was complimenting her on some attribute that he found pleasing. Why? "You like my propriety and my hobbies that I haven't even named. Which actually makes no sense."

His brow dropped low, his mouth pinching into a frown. "You're smarter than I thought you'd be."

"Thank you?" she said giving her head a small shake.

He waved. "No matter." Then he reached out to her again, taking her hand in his. Even with her gloves on, a tingly sort of sensation travelled up her arm. "What I wish to discuss with you, would solve all of your problems with the countess and with propriety and so on and so forth."

She lifted an eyebrow. "Why do I get the impression that I want to know the details of the so on and so forth?"

His mouth pulled to one side. "You ask a lot of questions."

"Again. Thank you." The tingling was growing distracting and so she pulled her hand from his. Then she bobbed another quick courtesy. "If that is all, my lord."

"No." He crossed his arms. "That isn't all."

She suppressed a sigh. He clearly wasn't going to gracefully allow her to leave until he'd said whatever he was hinting around. "Pray, continue."

He swallowed, his Adam's apple bobbing. "As a marquess there are certain duties that I need filled."

"Duties?" Oh dear. There was only one reason a lord wished to speak to a lady about his duties and that was when he wanted her to fulfill one of them for him by giving him a child. Cordelia cleared her throat, pressing her hand to her stomach.

"Yes." He stepped a bit closer and she moved back. The frown lines on his forehead deepened. "I am in need of a wife and child to ensure that my line and legacy continue. I think that you'd make an excellent candidate. Not only would you be helping me secure my future but I, in turn could protect you from any scandal."

"Scandal you're creating now by the two of us being here alone?" she asked, taking another step back. The Marquess of Malicorn was not a suitable candidate for her. Not only was he mysteriously dangerous, but he engaged in questionable past times.

He scoffed, the smell of the cigar he'd surely just smoked, filling her nostrils. She'd always liked the scent. It was earthy with a bit of cherry. "I mean you coming into a part of town you weren't supposed to be in and then stumbling into the back room of a gentleman's club." He lowered his head. "The countess knows sensitive information about you."

Cordelia placed her other hand over her heart. "Are all your friends going to propose to my sisters and cousin?" Point in fact, Minnie had just married the Duke of Darlington and the Earl of Exmouth had seemed quite interested in her sister Diana. Was this a group plan?

He raised his hands up. "What does that have to do with anything?"

"I'm just trying to determine your motivations. Your sudden proposal is quite a surprise."

He pinched the bridge of his nose with his thumb and two fingers. "Perhaps my first impression of you was incorrect."

"Oh, this should be interesting. Tell me, what did you think of me?" Butterflies flitted in her stomach exposing her lie. She wasn't entirely certain she wanted to know.

He dropped his hands. "That you'd be a suitable wife. I wished to speak with you to ask you to marry me."

"But you no longer wish to ask?" That was besides the point. She didn't want to marry him either. "And what about me precisely seemed suitable?" Even the word suitable made her heart sink. Diana was bold and daring. Minnie was strong and fiery. Grace was beautiful beyond compare and Ada was angelic. But Cordelia, the word burned in her brain. She was suitable. It wasn't that she hadn't known her entire life she was the least of all her

cousins and sisters. But she'd hoped, perhaps fool-
ishly, to find a man who thought her more. In fact, it
had been the one dream that had carried her
through a childhood where she was often unseen,
surrounded by so many beautiful women.

"You're not so loud and brash. You have manners,
you seem quiet and--"

"Please, Lord Malicorn. That's enough." She held
up her hand. "Much as I appreciate your offer for a
suitable match. I simply must decline."

"What?" He reached for her arm again but she
was quick enough to step back this time. She
wouldn't be caught by him again.

Taking a breath, she notched her chin as Diana or
Minnie would do. "You heard me, my lord. My
answer to your proposal is no."

Want to read more? Marquess of Malice

Read the entire Lords of Scandal series!

Duke of Daring
   Marquess of Malice
   Earl of Exile
   Viscount of Vice
   Baron of Bad
   Earl of Sin

Seeds of Love: Prequel to the Lily in Bloom series

Lily in Bloom

Midnight Magic

Keep up with all the latest news, sales, freebies, and releases by joining my newsletter!

www.tammyandresen.com

Hugs!

OTHER TITLES BY TAMMY

Boxed sets!!

Taming the Duke's Heart Books 1-3

Taming the Duke's Heart Books 4-6

A Laird to Love Books 1-3

A Laird to Love Books 4-6

Wicked Lords of London Books 1-3

Wicked Lords of London Books 4-6

Wicked Lords of London

Earl of Sussex

My Duke's Seduction

My Duke's Deception

My Earl's Entrapment

My Duke's Desire

My Wicked Earl

New: Taming the Duke's Heart
Taming a Defiant Duke
Taming a Wicked Rake
Taming an Unrepentant Earl
Taming my Christmas (Coming in November of 2019)

How to Reform a Rake
How to Reform a Rake
Don't Tell a Duke You Love Him
Meddle in a Marquess's Affairs
Never Trust an Errant Earl
Never Kiss an Earl at Midnight
Make a Viscount Beg

Brethren of Stone
The Duke's Scottish Lass
Scottish Devil
Wicked Laird
Kilted Sin
Rogue Scot
The Fate of a Highland Rake

A Laird to Love
Christmastide with my Captain (FREE!!!)
My Enemy, My Earl
Heart of a Highlander

A Scot's Surrender
My Laird's Seduction
The Earl's Forsaken Bride

Taming the Duke's Heart
Taming a Duke's Reckless Heart (FREE!! Check it out today!)
Taming a Duke's Wild Rose
Taming a Laird's Wild Lady
Taming a Rake into a Lord
Taming a Savage Gentleman
Taming a Rogue Earl

Made in the USA
Coppell, TX
10 March 2021

51569496R00127